**Swallowing hard, Dylan examined what he was feeling for the woman who had saved his nephew's life.**

The television caught his attention. The reporter was talking about Paige's amazing rescue this morning. Captivated and horrified all at the same time, he couldn't tear his eyes away from the woman who stood in front of the school where it had all happened giving a detailed account of the near miss.

In his mind, he watched it all over again as Paige's bike flashed in front of the car, her arm snaking out to grab Will and then the front headlight of the car clipping her back wheel. And down she went.

He sucked in a lungful of air.

Not knowing where the sensation came from, he couldn't help feeling his life was getting ready to be rocked by the woman lying on the bed upstairs.

## Books by Lynette Eason

Love Inspired Suspense

## *LYNETTE EASON*

grew up in Greenville, South Carolina. Her home church, Northgate Baptist, had a tremendous influence on her during her early years. She credits Christian parents and dedicated Sunday school teachers for her acceptance of Christ at the tender age of eight. Even as a young girl, she knew she wanted her life to reflect the love of Jesus.

Lynette attended the University of South Carolina in Columbia, South Carolina, then moved to Spartanburg, South Carolina, to attend Converse College, where she obtained her master's degree in education. During that time, she met the boy next door, Jack Eason, and married him. Jack is the executive director of the Sound of Light Ministries. Lynette and Jack have two precious children—Lauryn and Will. She and Jack are members of New Life Baptist Fellowship Church in Boiling Springs, South Carolina, where Jack serves as the worship leader and Lynette teaches Sunday school to the four- and five-year-olds.

# Agent
## Undercover

## LYNETTE EASON

*Love*Inspired

 LOVE INSPIRED BOOKS

Recycling programs for this product may not exist in your area.

ISBN-13: 978-0-373-67473-2

AGENT UNDERCOVER

Copyright © 2011 by Lynette Eason

www.LoveInspiredBooks.com

Printed in U.S.A.

The LORD is my light and my salvation—whom shall I fear? The LORD is the stronghold of my life—of whom shall I be afraid?

—*Psalms* 27:1

To my sweet parents, Lewis and Lou Jean Barker,
who support me in all that I do. I love you!

# ONE

Undercover Drug Enforcement Agent Paige Ashworth, known as Paige Worth in the little town of Rose Mountain, North Carolina, realized she had only seconds to act or the child would be dead. Shoving her right foot down on the bicycle pedal, she ignored her pounding heart and the desperate fear that said she didn't have enough time.

The little boy stood frozen in the middle of the school's crosswalk, eyes locked on the approaching vehicle. Time slowed until everything blurred except the child.

The crossing guard yelled something and, from the corner of her eye, Paige saw the man to her left bolt toward the terrified boy. The agonized expression on his face revealed that he knew he wouldn't make it in time.

"Will!" The hoarse scream tore from his throat, echoing in the air.

Doing her best not to think about the danger, she pedaled furiously, weaving in and out of the few stragglers still on the sidewalk, and swept into the crosswalk. The sun beat down in her eyes as the car's engine screamed in her ears, warning her she would lose this game of chicken.

But she had to try.

Paige could feel the heat radiating from the vehicle as she reached out to snag the boy around his waist. She knew she would be off balance and would probably hit the ground. Her only thought was to get clear of the car.

In spite of the muscles screaming in her right arm with the weight of the boy, she felt elation sweep through her.

She'd made it. Then something clipped her back wheel.

The bicycle handlebar lurched from her one-handed grasp and she lost control.

Felt herself going down.

Saw the ground coming up.

And twisted at the last minute so she was the one who crashed first, the child's body slamming onto her.

A sharp pain lanced the back of her head and then blackness descended.

Doctor Dylan Seabrook shook with fear and adrenaline. "Will!"

He raced to his nephew and grabbed him from his prone position on top of the woman who'd just saved Will's life. Dropping to his knees beside her, he did his best to assess the damage as quickly as possible.

She wasn't moving, her face white like death, blond hair splayed on the ground. But he could see her breathing. With one hand, he felt for a pulse under her chin, even as his other ran over Will's small frame checking for injuries.

He looked up at the nearest person. "Has someone called 911?"

"I did," a voice said to his left.

One person at a time, Dylan told himself. He gave Will a more thorough check and breathed a grateful sigh that he appeared physically unhurt, but the blank stare sent fear racing through Dylan. Will hadn't spoken in over eight weeks. Ever since his mother had died in a house fire. What would this do to him?

But he couldn't think about that now. The woman was hurt. Again, he glanced at Will. The boy just watched him with no expression on his face. Dylan grabbed his hand and pulled him down next to him. "Sit here, buddy, all right?"

Obedience, but no other response.

Switching to doctor mode, he glanced at the second hand on his watch while he took the woman's pulse. Steady and strong. Relief hit him.

As did the fact that she was undeniably beautiful. Beautiful and hurt.

He'd not only seen her head crack against the asphalt, he'd heard it. Just the memory of it made him sick. Why hadn't she been wearing a helmet? With one hand, he lifted each lid, noting the startling blue of her eyes even as he professionally assessed her pupils. One big, one small. A concussion.

A siren screamed in the distance. He placed a hand under her head to feel for a bump—and felt a warm wetness.

Pulling his hand away, he wiped the blood on his jeans. A brief thought that he should have waited until he had gloves flashed through his mind, but he dismissed it. The woman had saved Will's life. He would do whatever he had to do to save hers.

Sounds rushed at him, and he realized people were gathering around them in a crush. "Hey, move back and let her breathe, will you?"

Several people complied. But the concerned conversations buzzed around him like a swarm of bees.

Startled, he watched his nephew reach out and touch the woman's hand then slip his small fingers into her palm.

Emotion gripped Dylan's throat and wonder exploded through him. But he didn't have to time to think about what Will's reaching out to her meant.

Dylan wanted to examine the wound on the

back of her head, but didn't want to turn her neck. He ran his hands down her arms, his gaze once again drawn to Will's small hand in hers. Then back to business. Scrapes, bruises, a couple of gashes but nothing broken. He repeated his inspection on her legs. Same story.

His heart started to slow. No broken bones.

He glanced at her white face. No doubt along with the bad concussion, she'd have an even worse headache. Hopefully, that would be the extent of her injuries except for a few bumps and bruises.

The sirens continued to grow closer until the ambulance came into view.

A man stood in the street directing traffic. Two police cars pulled up and one of the officers took over. The other approached, a frown on his face. Spying Dylan, recognition dawned. "What happened, Doc?"

"Hey, Franco. She saved Will's life and got hit by a car for her trouble. The car kept going. Never put on the brakes, I don't think."

"Anybody get a plate?"

"I don't know. I know I didn't."

"I'm going to start taking statements."

Dylan acknowledged him with a nod and felt for her pulse one more time.

The paramedics pushed their way through the crowd, and Dylan recognized Lisa Bell and her partner, Sam Clark. Dylan told them, "We need a neck collar. She wasn't wearing a helmet and she took a hard hit to the head. Her pulse is steady, and there are no broken bones that I could feel."

The paramedics got to work on her. Soon she was ready for transport, and Dylan watched them load her up to be transported to the hospital about thirty minutes away in Bryson City.

Turning, he asked, "Who is she? Does anyone know?"

"Her name's Paige Worth."

Dylan eyed the man who'd spoken. Principal Tom Bridges. "Does she have any family that we can contact?"

Tom frowned and gave a shrug. "I don't know. I'll see who she listed on her application as an emergency contact. Today was supposed to be her first day on the job. She's my new guidance counselor."

The ambulance screamed off, and Dylan picked Will up to hold him and hopefully offer the child some comfort. "Okay." He studied his nephew. "I think Will is okay, but I'm going to take him to the hospital just to make sure, maybe have a couple of X-rays. I'll check on Ms. Worth while I'm there." He pulled a card out of his wallet and handed it to the man. "I know you can get my number from Will's file, but this will be easier. Please call and let me know who her contact person is." Dylan swallowed. "I want to talk to him or her."

Compassion lit the man's eyes. "Sure."

Dylan headed back to his house for his car, feeling Will's slight weight in his arms. Giving thanks for the life he held, a life that was almost cut short, he settled Will in his booster seat and wondered how he'd ever be able to pay Ms. Worth back for her selfless deed. He decided he'd pick up her totaled bike and keep it for her in case she wanted to salvage it for parts. He made a quick call to Principal Bridges, who assured Dylan that he'd hold the bike for him.

He started the car and pulled into the street. "Hey, Will, you all right, bud?"

Will simply met his eyes in the rearview mirror. Dylan sighed, wondering when the child would decide to speak. But even Will's counselor couldn't offer him a time frame. She just said they had to give him his space and time to heal.

Dylan noticed the car on his rear bumper. A car that looked suspiciously like the one that had almost hit Will. Dylan pressed the brake and slowed, giving the car the opportunity to go around him.

Instead, the vehicle slowed to keep the same amount of distance between them.

His pulse sped up and he swallowed hard.

Was he being followed?

Dylan put on his blinker and moved into the right-hand lane.

The car behind him did the same.

Sweat pooled on his forehead as Dylan considered his options. He took a right at the next block.

So did his tail.

The dark tint to the windshield prevented him from getting a good look at the driver, but it was definitely a male. He glanced at Will. The boy was oblivious to the possible danger, simply gazing out his window, trusting his uncle knew what he was doing.

Dylan flexed his fingers on the wheel and made the next turn that would take him to the police station two blocks away.

And the car behind him sped away.

There was no way to get a license number. He pulled into the police station parking lot and turned the car off.

Pulling a napkin from the glove compartment, Dylan wiped the sweat off his face and gathered his thoughts.

Should he go in and report the incident?

What incident? he mocked himself. Someone followed you a little too close, then turned off.

But the car resembled the one from this morning.

"It was white."

Will looked at him with a frown, and Dylan realized he'd spoken the words aloud. With a sigh and a prayer, Dylan turned the key in the ignition and pulled out of the parking lot. His eyes swept the surrounding area and didn't notice the white car waiting on him.

The tension in his shoulders released its grip and he relaxed a bit. "Sorry for the winding route, Will. I just had to check something out."

The little boy didn't respond other than to rub his eyes as though tired.

Dylan may have decided not to report the incident, but knew he wouldn't forget it.

Pain. That was her first thought. Her first feeling. Her first moment of awareness.

It felt like shards of glass biting into her skull with relentless determination. Her eyelids fluttered, and she thought she saw someone seated on the chair next to her.

Why was she in bed?

Memories flitted back. Bits and pieces. A little boy. A school. A crosswalk. A speeding car.

And she'd pedaled like a madwoman to dart in front of the car to rescue the child.

A gasp escaped her and she woke a little more. The pain faded to a dull throb. Where was the little boy? Was he all right?

Cool wetness touched her lips, and she jolted to

realize how thirsty she was. Greedily, she gulped at the water.

Awareness struggled into full consciousness, and she opened her eyes. Light filtered in around the closed curtains, and she squinted, her head sending warning signals.

Instead of listening, Paige pried her eyes fully open to stare into one of the most beautiful faces she'd ever seen. Aquamarine eyes crinkled at the corners, and full lips curved into a smile. She wanted to respond but was scared the movement would bring back the pounding pain.

The lips spoke. "Hello. Welcome back."

Another sweet face pushed its way into her line of sight. A little boy about six years old. Solemn blue eyes stared at her. His lips didn't smile, but a lone wrinkle on his forehead alerted her that he was worried about her.

With an effort, Paige forced her lips to curve upward. "Hi," she whispered.

The wrinkle smoothed, and she thought she saw the beginnings of a smile before it disappeared.

The hand over hers squeezed. "You saved Will's life, you know."

She had? Will. The little boy had a name. "Oh. Good." Her smiled slipped into a frown. "I was afraid I couldn't do it. That car…" She licked her lips, and the man reached over Will's head to pick up the cup. He held the straw to her lips, and she took a long swallow.

"Thanks."

He set the cup back down. "I'm Dylan Seabrook. This is my nephew, Will Price."

The name jolted her. Doing her best to keep her expression neutral, she simply smiled at him. She wanted to nod but didn't dare. "Hello, Dylan, Will." She focused on the boy. "I'm so glad you're all right."

"And he is, thanks to you. I tried…" He swallowed hard. "There's no way I would have been able to reach him in time. The crossing guard gave the all clear. Every day, I stand on the sidewalk and watch him cross to the waiting teacher who leads that group into the school." His voice had a raspy sound to it, and she realized he was doing his best to keep his emotions from overflowing.

Closing her eyes, Paige could see the racing car coming closer, hear the roar of the engine…

She flicked her eyelids up. "Did they catch him? Whoever was in the car?"

Dylan shook his head. "No. He—or she—never stopped. And we were all so focused on getting you help that no one even got the license number."

She sighed. "Well, I'm glad Will is okay. That's all that really matters."

"Why didn't you have a helmet on?"

Paige couldn't stop the flush that crept up her neck. Quite sure her cheeks were a rosy red, she said, "Because I—" She cut her eyes to the child who watched her with such a solemn expression. "I should have. It was very irresponsible of me not to have the helmet on. I got in a hurry and didn't grab it and then didn't want to go back and get it." She grimaced. "I won't make that mistake again. So—" she fingered the IV in her left arm "—when do I get to get out of here?"

"We'll go tell the doctor you're awake." He took the boy's hand. "Come on, buddy."

But Will pulled his hand from his uncle's and slid it into Paige's. Shock darkened Dylan's eyes, then they brightened and she thought she saw a flash of…hope?

"Will?"

But Will didn't budge. Paige smiled around the sharp throb of the headache that had started to put in an appearance. "He's fine. He can stay with me if he wants to."

Uncertainty flickered on his face, then he shrugged. "I'll only be a minute."

Paige breathed in and took a moment to wonder if her cover was blown. Her boss wasn't sitting in her hospital room, so that was a good thing. Her mother may have been contacted, but she wouldn't show up. A pang of hurt zipped through her before she could throw up the barrier that normally kept those kinds of thoughts at bay.

She'd given up on a relationship with her mom at the young age of eighteen when she'd left home to find her way. After a rocky start, she'd finally landed at the police academy and worked her way into her current position.

An agent with the Drug Enforcement Agency. Based in Atlanta, Georgia, she was on call for the state of North Carolina, too.

Being away from home didn't bother her. There really wasn't anything for her to miss. Her best friend was her job.

But a tiny part of her admitted she was lonely.

The small hand in hers squeezed, reminding her that she wasn't alone right now. A small shot of warmth coursed through her, and she squeezed back.

"So, Will, how old are you?"

He simply blinked.

"Hmm…don't want to talk, huh? Well, that's okay, I guess I'm still a bit of a stranger, aren't I? Maybe you can just nod?"

The door opened before she could continue the one-sided conversation, and Will's uncle entered, followed by the doctor and a nurse.

The dark-headed man smiled and said, "I'm Doctor Land. Glad to see you're awake." His chocolate eyes smiled at her.

"Thank you. So, when can I leave?"

"You had a pretty hard conk on the head." He consulted her chart. "I think we need to keep you for the night, just for observation."

Paige grimaced. "I have a job I need to get started on."

He was already shaking his head before she finished the sentence. "No, ma'am. You're in great shape physically, so the healing process should be pretty quick for you, but no working for a few days until we make sure there's nothing else going on with your head. We went ahead and did a CAT scan, and everything look okay, but head wounds are tricky. You need to take care."

"She will."

At Dylan's bold statement, Paige blinked at him. "Excuse me?"

He swallowed and flushed. "Sorry, I didn't meant to sound like I had any right to tell you what to do, it's just that—" he shuffled his feet and shoved his hands into his pockets "—I feel a little responsible and just want to…um…help. Will you let me?"

Unsure how to respond, Paige simply looked at him. She racked her brain for an appropriate response, but she couldn't very well tell him the real reason she needed to get to the school and get started in her job as guidance counselor. "I…uh… sure. I guess."

A smile finally crossed Will's little lips, and his grip tightened once again. She hadn't realized he still held her hand. He was so *quiet.* Not like other kids his age she'd been around. And she'd been around a lot during the training that taught her how to question children exposed to trauma.

"So, you want to take care of me, huh, Will?"

A nod so slight she thought she might have imagined it moved his head.

A sharp, indrawn breath from the boy's uncle made her glance his way. Shock and joy stood out on his handsome face making her wonder what was going on.

"Hmm. Well, let me think about it and I'll let you know." She had to contact Charles and let him know that she was okay. He'd be chomping at the bit at the fact that she hadn't checked in with him in over a day. She wondered how many voice messages he'd left on her phone.

The doctor flipped her chart closed. "There's a whole army of reporters outside wanting to talk to you. Apparently, someone called the local news."

For the first time since she'd awakened, a chill of fear shot through her. She couldn't talk to reporters. Staying alive meant maintaining her cover and keeping her face out of the limelight.

If the wrong person found out what she was doing in the town of Rose Mountain, she would wind up as dead as her fellow agent and friend, Larry Bolin.

# TWO

Dylan had been so focused on the fact that Will had responded to a question that he almost missed the flash of…what?…that crossed her face at the mention of the reporters. Fear? Consternation? Something.

"You don't want to talk to the reporters?" he asked. "Everyone is saying what a hero you are."

A flush crept up her neck causing her white cheeks to pinken. "I'm not a hero. So, please, tell them just to go away."

He glanced at the doctor who shrugged and said, "Okay. I'll tell security to handle it. Now, let me check you out." He motioned for Dylan and Will to wait outside.

Dylan took Will's hand, and the boy finally let go of Paige's to follow him. Once outside the room, Dylan thought about the woman who'd saved Will's life.

And her reaction to the idea of talking to reporters. Most women that he knew would love to be in the limelight, talk about how they'd saved a child. And even if they didn't necessarily revel in the attention, they wouldn't mind giving an interview.

But not Paige.

Interesting. Curious. It made him want to ask her about it, find out why she didn't want to be in the spotlight.

The hair on the back of his neck tingled, and he looked up. Nobody in the hall looked like they had an interest in what he was doing. Still, he frowned. After the incident with the car, he was on edge.

He'd been stopped by several reporters since the accident but thought he'd given them enough of what they'd wanted. Another sweeping glance still didn't reveal any reason he should feel watched.

Uneasy, he pasted a smile on his face and said to Will, "How about we go grab a little snack and then come back to see Ms. Worth?"

Will's lips parted in a smile.

For the second time that day.

Dylan's heart flipped. Ever since Will's mother, Dylan's sister, Sandra, had been killed in the fire that ripped through her house, Will had become mute, haunted by nightmares that woke him, that caused the little boy to scream until he was hoarse. And that was the only time he ever made a sound. Even when he cried, his tears were silent.

Dylan had shortened his hours at the medical clinic, working only during Will's school time so he could be there to pick up the boy from school.

And Will always seemed glad to see him. But Dylan felt there was something he was missing, something he should be doing for Will. He just wished he could put his hands on what that something was.

Even the therapist Will had been going to seemed stumped at the child's continued silence.

They walked into the cafeteria and Will went straight to the fruit section. Dylan got him a bowl of grapes and banana slices, and they found a table in the corner. Will picked up his fork and stabbed a piece of banana.

Surprise hit Dylan when he found himself wanting to hurry Will up so they could go back to check on Paige.

Swallowing hard, he examined what he was feeling. He wasn't in a good place to be this attracted to someone. He had been engaged until very recently, but Dylan could finally admit that his and Erica's relationship had died long ago even though the recent betrayal still hurt.

Pushing those thoughts away, Dylan felt a smile curve his lips. It might be fun to get to know Paige. To see what she was all about.

To hear her deepest secrets.

Then he frowned. Of course if he expected that of her, he'd have to be willing to reciprocate.

Then he flushed, embarrassed by his premature thoughts. He'd just met the woman. He knew nothing about her. For all he knew, she might have a boyfriend somewhere. Someone who lived in another state and just hadn't come to be by her side.

The television caught his attention. The reporter was talking about Paige's amazing rescue this morning. Captivated and horrified all at the same time, he couldn't tear his eyes away from the woman who stood in front of the school where it had all happened giving a detailed account of the near miss.

In his mind, he watched it all over again as her bike flashed in front of the car, her arm snaked out to grab Will and then the front headlight clipped her back wheel. And down she went.

He sucked in a lungful of air.

Not knowing where the sensation came from, he couldn't help feeling his life was getting ready to be rocked by the strawberry blonde, blue-eyed woman lying on the bed upstairs.


As soon as the doctor stepped from the room, Paige grabbed the cell phone that had been placed on the table beside her. She punched in the number she'd memorized a long time ago.

Her boss answered on the second ring. "Ashworth," Charles Forester almost growled, "where are you? Are you all right? I just talked to 'your principal' who said you were in the hospital. What's going on?"

"I'm fine." Well, she would be. "But we've got a problem. Reporters have already gotten wind of the story and are making a big deal out of it."

Filling him in, she did her best to ignore the aching in her head compounded by his sudden bid for her to hold on.

She held.

A minute later, he said, "I'm back."

"I should be out of here tomorrow and plan on getting back to the school as soon as possible." She paused. "How's Larry's family doing?"

"Not good." His voice lowered. "They need his killer brought to justice, Paige."

"I'm working on it, but I need you to make sure that my face doesn't appear on the news. If some hotshot reporter or photographer decides to make this his story, and someone recognizes me…"

A long pause.

"Charles?"

"I'm watching the reports now. Got Louis to pull it up and stream it to my computer as soon as you said something about reporters." Louis, the DEA's tech guy who could do anything with a computer. "Right now, the story's only on the local channel. We'll do our best to keep it that way."

Paige blew out a sigh and shifted her head. "And you're still against working with the sheriff on this one?"

"Definitely. He's squeaky clean, but Larry's dead, and the investigation of his death hasn't produced much. Let's keep this one close to our vest for now. If we need to bring the sheriff into it, we will. I'm still screening his deputies."

Thoughtlessly, Paige nodded and grimaced at the shaft of pain that shot through her. Maybe she'd be out of commission a bit longer than she thought.

"All right, give me a couple of days, and I'll see how I feel. One more thing, you'll never guess who the little boy was."

"Who?"

"Dylan Seabrook's nephew, Will Price. Dylan was walking him to school when all this happened. Dylan always lets him cross to the guard who waits in the center of the street. He was almost to her when the car came flying down the street toward him."

Charles scoffed in disbelief. "You're kidding. Sandra Price's son? The woman who was killed in the fire with Larry?"

"Yes." She paused. "This accident may actually

be a blessing in disguise. It gives me a way to get close to Dylan."

A pause. "Are you sure it was an accident?"

She thought about it. "No, I'm not."

"If the people who killed Larry and Sandra think Dr. Seabrook knows something, they may decide he needs to disappear—or cause his nephew to in order to keep him quiet."

"I know." The thought filled her with dread. "I need to find out if he's had any threats made against him or Will."

"That sounds like a good place to start. Listen, I know you haven't had a chance to really work on the case yet, but given that you've been in the town for a couple of days, are you sure we've got you in the right place? The elementary school rather than the high school?"

"I think so, based on what Larry said about Sandra being friends with one of the parents who was arrested. Although she didn't know the name of the person who supplied the drugs—or exactly how they were being transported through the school—she was pretty adamant that they were coming from the elementary school. The ID found in the fire is the biggest sign, of course." A charred staff ID from Rose Mountain Elementary School had been found in the residue of the fire.

"And the drug dogs came up empty." He sighed. "All right then. Keep in mind, we've also got a detective questioning those two parents who were arrested for possession."

Paige pulled in a breath. "Great. As soon as I recover and do a little investigating, I'll be in touch."

"You'd better be."

"Bye."

"Oh, Ashworth."

"Yes?"

He cleared his throat. "Good job on saving the kid."

"Thanks, Charles."

"And keep in mind, there are major storm and tornado watches going on in your area. I know tornados in the mountains are rare, but not unheard of. Keep up with the weather."

"Will do."

She hung up the phone and set it back on the table.

Her brain whirled. Where to start? She looked around the room. A small bouquet of flowers sat near the sink. She had just now noticed them. A smile curved her lips. No doubt they were from Dylan and Will. Then she frowned. She didn't need to be having any warm, fuzzy feelings for the brother of the woman she was here to look into.

A knock on the door made her jump. By reflex,

her hand went for the weapon she normally carried in her shoulder holster. Only to come up empty.

Right. She hadn't wanted to carry the gun into the school, so she'd left it locked in her gun box in the drawer of her nightstand. But she didn't have any enemies here. She was simply a guidance counselor.

"Come in."

The door opened once again and a man Paige knew to be her new boss stepped in. The principal of Rose Mountain Elementary.

She offered him a weak smile. "Hello, Dr. Bridges." She'd met him briefly at the district office on the day of her interview two weeks ago. Only the superintendent of the school district, whose cooperation had been needed to secure Paige's position at the school as the new guidance counselor, knew the real reason she was in Rose Mountain.

"Please. Call me Tom. How are you feeling?"

"Like I cracked my head open."

He gave a laugh and, for the next few minutes, they continued the small talk. Then Tom asked, "Is there anyone I can call for you? A man named Charles answered the emergency number you listed on the application. Said he was your brother."

"Right. Thank you for contacting him." They'd agreed Charles would play the role of her brother if he ever needed to come see her during one of her undercover operations. Or if there was ever an emergency. Like this morning.

"Yes. He said to let him know if your condition worsened and he'd come."

Charles had been giving her time to call him and let him know whether she needed help or not. "I appreciate you doing that."

He stood. "Well, you take your time getting well. We'll see you when the doctor says you can come to work."

"Thank you."

After he left, she closed her eyes. In her mind, she pictured the agent who'd been killed in the fire with his informant—and girlfriend. Paige frowned at that. She wasn't sure she agreed with Larry's choice, but he'd been struck by the woman the moment he'd met her in the teacher's lounge of the high school.

The feeling had been mutual and Sandra Lee Price, Dylan's sister, had agreed to help the DEA put away as many people as possible that were involved in the drug ring that was suspected to be originating out of Rose Mountain.

And now she was dead, along with Larry, an excellent agent and Paige's good friend. She bit her lip to stem the tears.

Paige glanced at the door where Dylan and Will had disappeared a little while ago.

It was Paige's job to find out exactly how much Dylan knew about his sister's death. And if he was involved in any way.

# THREE

Dylan dropped Will off at school—this time walking him all the way to his classroom door—and headed for the hospital. He'd had a restless sleep the night before, and it was all thanks to the pretty blonde woman on the fifth floor saving Will's life over and over in his dreams. Her twisted bike waited in his garage.

Climbing out of his car, he loped to the front door and made his way upstairs.

The two ladies and one male nurse at the nurses' station waved as he passed. Walking down the hall, he slowed when he spied someone hanging around Paige's door. A relative? A friend?

A significant other?

Dylan was unsure whether to keep going or come back another time.

The guy hesitated, placed his hand on the doorknob, then pulled it back as though undecided whether he should enter the room or not. Dylan tried to get a look at his face, but the baseball cap shielded his features as he looked left, then right.

A funny feeling twisted inside Dylan. "Hey, can I help you?"

The man froze, ducked his head and started walking toward the exit. "No thanks, wrong room."

Dylan watched him push open the door to the stairs and disappear.

His suspicions increased. Something about the guy made alarm bells go off. He walked quickly to the end of the hall and looked into the stairwell. No one was visible.

Shaking his head and telling himself the man may very well have had the wrong room, Dylan decided not to make a big deal out of it. Although, he had to admit, his instincts continued to shout that something wasn't right.

Arriving at Paige's door, he pushed away the uneasy feeling, took a deep breath and wiped his damp palms down the sides of his khaki slacks.

Why was he so nervous?

Because he was attracted to Paige. He wanted her to like him. For the first time since his fiancée's desertion, he cared what a woman thought.

And he desperately wanted to keep her around to see her with Will again. She just might be the key to unlocking the boy's self-imposed silence. A mixture of self-disgust and humor at his befuddled state of mind nearly had him laughing. But he sobered up and knocked on the door.

"Come in."

He entered to find Paige pulling a brush through her hair as gently as possible. The bandage that had been on the back of her head yesterday was gone. He gulped at the zing of attraction that rippled through him. He hadn't just imagined her beauty. "At least they didn't have to shave it."

She gave a chuckle. "No. I think they were more worried about the effects of the bump than the small cut."

He frowned. "What are you doing up?"

"I'm going home." She wrinkled her nose. "And before you ask, yes, I feel up to it. I feel much better today than I did yesterday, that's for sure. No dizziness, still a slight headache, but no blurred vision. The doctor said to take it easy for a few days. I'm not at a hundred percent yet, but—" she shrugged "—I'm getting there." Changing the subject, she asked, "Where's your sidekick?"

Dylan smiled. "He's at school"

"No lasting side effects for him?"

"No. Not this time," he murmured.

She dropped her arm, the brush clutched in her right hand. "This time?"

Had he said that out loud?

"Will's mother, Sandra, was killed in a fire almost two months ago. He has nightmares about it from time to time. Last night was peaceful. I checked on him off and on all night, and he slept pretty well."

Concern clouded her pretty eyes. "Oh, I'm sorry to hear about his mother. How awful. What happened?"

Dylan set his jaw. "I'll tell you about it sometime. For now, do you need a ride?"

She cocked her head at him. "I was going to take a cab."

His smile reappeared. "All the way from Bryson City to Rose Mountain?"

She flushed. "Oh. How far away are we?"

"About thirty minutes."

"I guess I'm more used to big-city living than small-town."

"Which big city are you from?"

"Atlanta."

A soft whistle escaped him. "Wow, you're serious when you say big city, aren't you? What brought you to our little mountain town?"

A frown furrowed her forehead. "Let's just say I needed a change. The slower-paced lifestyle appeals to me."

Well, that was good news. That might mean she planned on staying for a while. He lifted a brow. "So? You want a ride?"

"Um…sure. Let me just get my things."

A knock sounded at the door and Dylan moved

to pull it open. A large man decked out in green scrubs pushed a wheelchair. He flashed her a bright smile. "Your limo is ready."

Paige frowned. "I don't need a chair."

"Hospital regulations, ma'am."

Dylan watched the frown slide off to be replaced with resignation. "Fine."

After she was settled, the three of them left the room. Dylan jogged ahead to get the car and pull it around.

Once Paige was in the passenger seat, Dylan asked, "Where am I going?"

She gave a little laugh—and winced.

He frowned. "Are you sure you're all right?"

"Yes, now stop asking. I live on Mockingbird Lane in Knightsbridge Subdivision."

He lifted a brow. "That's not too far from where Will and I live." A surge of elation slid through him at the idea of her living so close to him. Then he wondered why it mattered. But it did. The attraction he felt for her, the connection she seemed to have with Will—both excellent reasons for keeping her nearby.

"So, Dr. Seabrook, you didn't have to see patients today?"

Before he could answer, his cell phone rang. Grabbing it from the clip on his side, he said, "Hello?"

"Where are you, Dylan?" Margaret, his secretary and friend from church. They'd dispensed with formalities when he'd hired her after her husband had died of a massive heart attack.

He frowned. "Taking a friend home from the hospital. What's wrong?"

"I have a young man standing here who said you promised to meet him this morning to give him a reference letter."

Dylan racked his brain—and found what he was looking for. "I totally forgot. I have it all ready. I just need to print and sign it. Tell him if he can give me about thirty minutes, I'll be there."

"You got it. See you then."

He looked over at his passenger. "Is your head all right? Do you mind if we swing by my office when we get into town?"

She shrugged. "Fine with me."

"I promised a reference letter for a very promising young man in my church. He wants to get into medical school, and I think he'd make an excellent doctor."

Thirty-five minutes later, Dylan pulled into the parking lot and noticed one of his partners, Graham Bailey, hadn't arrived yet. The man was going through a pretty messy divorce and his days seemed to start later and later. Henry Satterfield, his other partner, would field patients until Graham arrived. Dylan had already requested time off to be with Will, so no one expected him to be there.

Dylan entered the building with Paige right behind him. Margaret Rogers, his efficient as always, salt-and-pepper-haired secretary in her early sixties sat at her desk fielding calls. She pointed to the young man sitting in the waiting room.

Two women with toddlers chatted in the children's corner. A teenager slumped on the couch, his hat pulled low over his eyes.

Dylan nodded and turned to speak when Margaret hung up the phone with more force than needed. He looked back at her. "What is it?"

"Doctor Bailey won't be in today. He's sick." She kept her expression clear, her voice in a monotone, but he could see the disgust in her eyes.

"Okay, let me take care of this, then I'll…figure something out about Graham." He made quick introductions. "Paige, Margaret Rogers and Kyle Barrett. Margaret and Kyle, this is Paige."

Kyle nodded. The women greeted each other while Dylan walked over to shake the man's hand. "Give me a minute, Kyle. The letter is sitting on my computer, I just need to print it off and sign it."

"Thank you, sir."

Kyle sat and Dylan made his way down the hall to his office.

Twisting the doorknob, he stepped inside and came to an abrupt halt.

In shock, he took in the mess that had been his spotless office less than twenty-four hours earlier.

The gasp behind him made him turn to see Paige staring over his shoulder. Then she looked up at him and raised a brow. "You either need to fire your cleaning crew or call the police."

Even after the sheriff arrived, Kyle hovered in the background, eyes wide like saucers. "Looks like the tornado sirens should have sounded."

While Paige watched the officer take notes on the scene, Margaret clucked like a mother hen, muttering under her breath. Paige listened to Dylan give a statement and clamped her teeth on her tongue. Itching to be a part of the investigation, she told herself to cool it. That wasn't going to happen.

But she couldn't help sidling up next to Dylan and asking, "Who would do this?"

He shook his head. "I have no idea. This is crazy." He gestured to the uniformed man. "Paige, this is a good friend of mine, Sheriff Eli Brody."

She nodded, then asked, "How did whoever did this get in?"

Eli shook his head. "We're working on figuring that out."

Margaret huffed. "Well, I'm usually the last to leave and I always set the alarm."

Dylan smiled at her. "No one is questioning your competence." He looked thoughtful and then shook his head.

Paige's gaze went back to the office. The overturned chair, the dumped drawers. "It looks like someone was looking for something."

"Sure does."

Dylan shrugged. "But what? Drugs? Any junkie would know they're not kept in an office."

"The drug cabinet wasn't touched as far as I can tell," Margaret offered. "I just checked."

Paige looked at Dylan. "Has anyone threatened you or Will?"

He blinked. "No. Why?"

Okay, that answered that question. "What about your prescription pads?"

Cocking his head, he looked at the sheriff. "Do you mind if I look?"

"I've already dusted the desk. Go ahead."

Dylan walked behind the desk, inserted a small key into the top drawer and gave the handle a tug. Looking in, he shook his head. "Everything's in order."

The sheriff blew out a sigh. "All right."

Paige's eyes bounced back and forth between the men. Would no one say it? She bit her lip. Should she bring it up?

"You…uh…don't suppose there's a connection between the car trying to run Will down and this break-in, do you?"

Both men looked startled. "Why would you ask that?"

She gave a sheepish shrug. "I don't know. I mean, I guess it's just weird that both things happened so close to each other."

Sheriff Brody looked thoughtful. His forehead wrinkled as he ran his hand through his thick dark hair. Intuitive green eyes examined his friend. "You got any enemies, Dylan?"

"No." He gave a humorless laugh. "No way. I mean, who would do something so awful as to actually try to run Will down?" He looked sick. "That's just…crazy."

"Crazier things have been done," Paige murmured.

He simply looked at her.

"Do you have any patients you've made mad recently?" the sheriff asked.

Dylan looked blindsided, she thought, even as she waited for his answer.

He gave a slow shake of his head. "I don't… know. Maybe."

"Could be you were the intended target with that car. The person who almost ran down Will could have thought you were going to be crossing with him," Paige said before she could bite her tongue.

Sheriff Brody crossed his arms across his broad chest and narrowed his eyes. "You have some law enforcement training?"

Paige gulped and chastised herself for making such a rookie mistake. She forced a laugh. "I watch a lot of television. Crime shows are my favorite."

His eyebrows lowered and he glowered. She could read his thoughts. Great, another cop wannabe.

One day she'd tell him the truth. For now, she was going to shut up. Besides, her head was really starting to pound. Nausea swirled and she knew she needed to lie down. "Dylan, do you think you could take me home now?"

He started. "Sure." Then looked at the sheriff. "Are you done with me?"

"Yeah." The man waved a hand in dismissal. "Go on. I'll let you know if we find anything here." He glanced at his watch. "I'm supposed to meet Holly at the doctor's office in Bryson City. We're having our first ultrasound." He looked extraordinarily pleased to share that information.

Paige smiled through her pain. "Congratulations."

"Thanks." He peered closer at Paige then said

to Dylan, "She's not looking so great. You better get some meds in her before she passes out."

Dylan turned and stopped fast enough to cause Paige to bump into him. Pain exploded through her. As it eased, with her nose buried in his back, she couldn't help noticing his yummy-smelling cologne. She backed up in a hurry and swallowed hard.

He turned and smiled down at her. "Sorry." Then he motioned for the young man who'd come to collect his reference letter. "I'm sorry, I can't access my computer right now. I have a copy of it on my home computer. Is it all right if we try again later?"

"Sure. You've got my cell number. Just give me a shout when you want me to come pick it up."

Dylan and Paige made their way out to his car. She slid in, breathing in the familiar scent of leather and new-car smell. The sun beat down, warming the interior of the car to an uncomfortable temperature. She lowered her window and he flipped on the air-conditioning. "Sorry to pull you away," she told him. "My head is really hurting."

"No problem. I wasn't doing anyone any good just standing around watching them work." He shot her a worried look. "Any nausea? Dizziness?"

"No, it's just a headache." The nausea had faded.

Red flashing lights jerked her attention to the side mirror. A fire truck approached, sirens screaming. Dylan's face paled, and his hands clenched the wheel so tight his knuckles went white. He pulled to the side and let the truck fly past. For a moment, he just sat there, not moving.

She laid a hand on his arm. "Are you okay?"

He blinked. "Yeah." His hoarse voice said otherwise. "Tell me how to find your house."

She gave him the directions, then asked, "That fire truck really sparked some memories, didn't it?"

"They always do. I can't see one without..." He broke off and swallowed.

"Will you tell me more about the fire that killed Will's mother?"

# FOUR

Eyes on the road, Dylan blinked at the question, then supposed it was only natural that she ask. Still, it threw him. Then again, she seemed to have some sort of connection with Will, so maybe it wasn't so odd she'd want to know more about the boy's mother. He gathered his scattered nerves and said, "Sandra was my sister. She was a good mom. Most of the time."

"I'm sorry for your loss, Dylan." She paused. "What do you mean most of the time?"

"She did drugs." Blunt, straight to the point.

"Oh, my. Poor Will."

"Yes. At first, it wasn't like she was an out of control junkie. She was more recreational than anything, but…" He bit his lip.

"She ended up hooked?"

He drew in a deep breath. "In a big way."

"I'm sorry."

"Me, too. Anyway, she had this new boyfriend that seemed to be making a big impact on her.

Larry something. He was a math teacher out at the high school. Sandra did a lot of subbing at all three schools in town. But I remember her coming over one night and telling me about this great guy. And she was going to change her life. I only met Larry a few times." A smile crossed his lips.

"What's the smile for?"

He shook his head. "Just thinking about the two of them. I was really skeptical when she first told me about him. Figured he was just another drug source, but he wasn't. I could tell he was clean the moment I met him, and he really did seem to care about Sandra. In fact, they reminded me of a couple of teenagers who'd just discovered true love."

"True love?" She sounded skeptical.

Dylan eyed her from the corner of his eye then asked softly, "What? You don't believe in true love?" He really didn't have the right to ask, but he wanted to know. Even though his experience with Erica had cut deep, he still felt like God had the right person in mind for him.

He couldn't help wondering if that person was Paige.

He could feel her embarrassment as she cleared her throat. "Maybe. For some people."

"But not for you?"

A pause. "This isn't about me," she finally answered, sounding subdued. "So Sandra and Larry were in love?"

Making a mental note to come back to her feelings about love, he let her direct him back to the topic. "I don't know, but Sandra finally seemed happy. Like she'd gotten rid of a few of her demons. Larry even got her going to church. And Will was crazy about the guy…" He sighed. "But I just…don't know… It was hard for me to hope because…she was still Sandra, you know?"

"Yeah. I know."

Dylan glanced at her. "You sound like you mean that. Is someone you love a drug addict?"

Paige flinched and he reached over to touch her shoulder. The warm zing that skittered up his arm surprised him. "I'm sorry. I didn't mean to find a painful subject. Are you okay?"

She placed a hand to her head. "Um, yes, just a headache. I'll take one of those painkillers as soon as I get home and sleep for a couple of hours. That should do the trick."

Dylan frowned at her but let that explanation work for now. He had a feeling she'd been going to say something else and had decided against it. He didn't let it bother him. He usually wasn't so open with people he'd only just met, but there was just something about Paige, something that made him want to explore the possibility of a relationship.

Plus, he had Will to think of. What if Will's reaction to Paige was just a fluke? Then again, what if it wasn't? Their connection seemed real.

He had to keep Paige around in order to find out. Of course, with the way he was attracted to her, it was obvious that wasn't going to be a hardship. At least not for him.

He cut those thoughts off as she directed him to turn into the drive of a small, yet cozy-looking house with gray vinyl siding and green shutters. "Ah, you rented this from the Jacksons, didn't you?"

"Yes. My...brother found it for me."

"Well, I know they're relieved to have it rented. They've had some serious financial difficulties since he was laid off six months ago. Rose Mountain is a great little town, but unfortunately, it doesn't offer much in the way of employment unless you have a specialty."

"Like medicine?"

He smiled. "Like medicine—or teaching. Or owning your own business." He turned the engine off and started to climb out.

"You don't have to get out. I can make it."

He knew she could, but for some reason he wasn't ready to say goodbye to her yet. "Do you mind if I see you in? Make sure you have everything you need?"

She narrowed her eyes and he held his breath until she said, "Sure. Thanks."

The joy that stirred in his heart didn't shock him at this point, but it did make him remind himself to take it easy. His heart ignored the reminder and thumped faster.

He followed Paige up the steps to the covered porch. She slid the key in the lock and opened the door. "My garage door opener is in the car." She froze. "My bike! I totally forgot to ask anyone about it."

Dylan grimaced. "I'm afraid it was pronounced dead at the scene." He flushed. "But I told Principal Bridges I would keep it at my house until you could decide what you wanted to do with it. The dump is probably the best place for it."

She eyed him and he squirmed under her gaze. She asked, "It's that bad?"

"Trust me. It's that bad."

She sighed. "Okay. I'll come by and take a look at it when I'm feeling a little better."

A bush rustled to her left and she shot a glance over her shoulder. Visions of the car speeding into the school crosswalk flashed momentarily, and she blinked.

Another rustle. An animal? A neighbor child playing hide-and-seek?

Dylan must have heard it, too, as he turned to look at the bush.

She tensed. Or something more sinister?

The bush shook and she heard—a sneeze?

She moved toward the sound. "Whoever you are, you better come out now, or I'm calling the police."

Absolute stillness.

Paige narrowed her eyes. Was she being paranoid? Dylan walked up the steps of the porch and grabbed the broom she'd left next to the door.

Coming back down, he flipped it so the handle pointed toward the shrubbery.

Paige's adrenaline rushed through her as he poked into the bush.

A grunt sounded. "Ouch! Stop!"

Tempted to run inside and grab her gun, she ignored the feeling. Instead, she pulled out her cell phone. "You have two seconds to show yourself or I'm calling the cops. I—"

"All right, all right." The voice sounded frustrated. Then a head popped around the side of the bush. "Paige Worth?"

A young man in his mid-thirties with shaggy blond hair gradually revealed himself. He had a smile on his face that Paige immediately didn't trust. He looked—*oily* was the word that popped into her head.

Dylan didn't look like he was too happy to see the guy, either.

Paige narrowed her eyes and drilled him with a

harsh glare. "Why are you hiding in my bushes?" she asked.

The trespasser rubbed his chin and studied her. She saw his eyes settle on the bandage around her head. "Aren't you the one who saved the little boy yesterday?"

"Again, who are you and why were you in my bushes?" Paige responded without answering the question.

The man held out a hand. "I'm Simon Moore. A reporter for the *Bryson City Journal.*" Paige shook his hand and felt her insides cool.

His eyes zeroed in on Dylan, and Paige watched Dylan narrow his eyes at the man. "And you're the doctor, right? The little boy's dad?"

"Uncle," Dylan replied.

A "gotcha" look appeared in the reporter's eyes, and Paige grimaced at Dylan's slip. He'd just confirmed that the reporter had the right people. "I'm sorry about the hiding thing. You didn't want to talk in the hospital and I thought I could—"

"—convince me to talk to you by ambushing me outside my home?" Paige raised a brow in disbelief. The man didn't even have the grace to look embarrassed.

"Look," Dylan said before Mr. Moore could open his mouth again. "She's still not feeling well and needs to get inside and rest. Why don't you come back another time?"

"Actually, don't bother. There's not a story here, all right? Please." Paige softened her tone. "I have a headache and want to lie down. Feel free to report what happened, just leave me out of it."

"Why?" A calculating look crossed his face as he assessed Paige, then Dylan. "Do you two have something to hide?"

Paige drew in a pained breath. "No, Mr. Moore, we don't have anything to hide. Will is a little boy who needs a little less excitement in his life. I simply…" She trailed off. "It doesn't matter, does it? You're just going to write what you want." She gave a snort of disgust. "Happy reporting."

She stepped inside, and Dylan followed after one last look at the reporter who stood sideways, speaking into his little voice-activated recorder before stomping toward the car Dylan just now noticed parked two houses down.

Once inside, Dylan shut the door behind him. "He looks familiar."

Her eyes drilled into his and he raised a brow. She asked, "Where have you seen him before?"

"I think he was the guy standing outside your hospital room earlier."

"What guy?"

Dylan thought she looked pale, and he wondered if it was from the pain in her head or the thought of the reporter. She definitely hadn't been interested in any media attention at the hospital. He couldn't help it that a small part of him wondered if maybe she *did* have something to hide. His gut twisted at the thought. "When I came to see if you needed a ride earlier, there was someone standing outside your door. I asked him if I could help him and he said he had the wrong room."

She stood perfectly still, thinking hard about something. Dylan wondered what was going on inside her head.

"What did he look like?"

Shaking his head, Dylan squinted as he thought. "I'm not sure. He had on jeans and a green polo shirt. A ball cap covered his head and face. I didn't get a good look at him."

Paige's eyes met his and he could tell she was processing this information. "That guy had on jeans and a green polo shirt but no ball cap. I'm willing to bet that's not a coincidence."

Dylan shook his head. "He was probably hoping to catch you alone in the hospital to try and get a story out of you." Shrugging, he gave her a smile. "Anyway, I'm relieved you're not interested in doing the story for that reporter."

"It's no problem. I'm not into that kind of thing."

"You're right about Will. He has been through enough. He doesn't need all the excitement a story and pictures in the newspaper would bring."

She smiled. "Then I'm glad I told him no."

Dylan pulled his gaze from the beautiful woman in front of him, put the reporter out of his mind and glanced around. They were in the family room. A breakfast nook and kitchen lay to the left. "Nice place. You haven't decorated much, but it's a very functional, open layout."

She laughed. "No, I haven't gotten to the decorating part yet, and I just thought the layout was cute."

"Well, that too, but real men don't use the word *cute* in reference to a house."

Another laugh, followed by a wince. "Don't. It hurts to be amused right now." She settled on the couch and leaned her head back.

"You need to be resting and can't do that if you're hurting. Where are the pain pills the doctor prescribed? I'll get them for you."

"In my purse, but I can get them."

"You just stay put, I'll take care of it." He grabbed her purse from the kitchen counter where it had landed after her careless toss. Walking over to the couch, he handed it to her.

"Thank you, *darling*."

He jerked at the familiar term then caught the teasing glint in her eyes and the impish smile on her lips. Another flush worked its way up his neck, and he shook his head as he realized how his actions had come across. "Sorry, I don't mean to act so…"

"Husbandly?" The word hung between them, then Paige groaned. He noted her red cheeks as she opened the purse. She said, "Okay, I obviously have brain damage. Or am in desperate need of some sleep. I'm going to take some medicine and get some rest." He watched her cover her embarrassment by rising from the couch, and heading for the kitchen. She kicked off her shoes in the middle of the room and gave them a halfhearted shove as though to move them out of the way.

Dylan heard her rummaging in the refrigerator and thought about that word.

Husbandly.

Pain kicked him in the heart. He'd almost been a husband. And then he'd gotten custody of Will. Erica, his fiancée, had decided she didn't want a package deal and dumped him the day Will came to live with him. The day after the fire.

He focused on Paige. "Do you need any help? Anything to eat?"

She came to the door of the kitchen looking incredibly cute—he felt fine using that word in reference to her—with her bare feet, hair around her shoulders and not a touch of makeup on. He finally noticed her height. She was about five inches shorter than his own six foot two. She offered him a water bottle and he took it.

"No, thanks. I'm not hungry right now. I'll get something when I wake up." Popping a little white pill in her mouth, she took a swig from her bottle and motioned him into the den area. As she headed that way, she stepped on one of her shoes and almost tripped.

Moving fast, Dylan caught her by the upper arm and pulled her against him. Water sloshed from the bottle and caught him on the chin. Wide, green eyes blinked up at him. "Oops. I'm so sorry!" She glanced at her shoes. "That'll teach me not to pick up after myself." A warm hand reached up and wiped the water from his chin.

Dylan swallowed hard as he found himself entranced, speechless and very aware of the warmth of her. His gaze dropped to her lips and, for a brief second, he considered seeing what she would do if he kissed her.

She caught her breath and stepped back. His arms dropped. Then Paige wiggled her fingers at him and said, "I think you need a towel. I'm not doing much good."

Clearing his throat, he shook his head. "I'm fine." He wiped his chin on his shirt and smiled at the flush on her cheeks. So, these feelings catching him off guard weren't one-sided. That was good to know.

Dylan walked toward the couch. "Are you sure you don't want me to get out of your hair so you can rest?"

Lying down and closing her eyes sounded wonderful. She'd pushed herself too hard today and was feeling the effects of it. However, Paige was determined to get some answers first—and push away the delicious feeling of being in his arms. Not that it was surprising that she'd enjoyed being there considering her instant attraction to the man. What surprised her was the desire to get to know him better on a personal level, not just in conjunction with her job.

And because of that desire, she had to tread carefully. Find out what she could about the fire and his sister, before she could even admit she was interested in him.

She had about twenty minutes before the pain pill would kick in.

"In a few minutes. Please, sit."

He did, watching her with that concerned look on his face that made her do things she hadn't done in a really long time. Like giggle. Really, what was up with that?

Paige told herself to focus on what he had to tell her—not the fact that he was looking better and better every minute she spent in his presence. She still had to rule him out as a suspect for the fire that had killed her friend and fellow agent.

And his sister.

But his background check had come back clean. She was here simply checking up on him as a formality. The fact that he had acted to save her life after her collision with the car, the fact that he was straight-up honest with her about his sister's drug use and the fact that he didn't seem to have a deceptive bone in his body had her convinced he'd had nothing to do with the fire.

But she'd press on with a few more questions and confirm her beliefs. As much as she would like to go with her gut, she needed some hard evidence that said he was innocent of any wrongdoing. Paige hated this deception, the lying to him, the constant watching of her words around him. She shoved the feeling aside.

Deception was the nature of the career she'd chosen and she'd do it well.

"So…" she settled on the other end of the couch "…what happened that night? I'd ask how Will is handling it, but I guess that's pretty obvious."

Grief clouded his eyes and she felt a pang of guilt for poking around memories that weren't that old and were obviously painful. But she had to.

It was her job and she needed to find Larry's killer. But she couldn't help offering, "I can see the pain in your eyes. You don't have to tell me if you don't want to." Biting her lip, she continued her role. "But I'm going to be working with Will at school. It might help me with him if I know some of the story." She'd prefer the whole thing, but would take what she could get for now.

Pulling in a deep breath, Dylan rubbed a hand over his eyes and said, "Whatever Will saw scared him enough—traumatized him enough—that he hasn't said a word since."

Paige winced. "I'm sorry."

"So am I." He looked down at his hands. "Sandra, my sister, and her boyfriend, Larry, were at home when the fire started. I don't know why they couldn't get out." His words slowed. "At first, I thought Sandra must have been smoking something and it was her fault the fire started, but the autopsy report showed she was clean."

"Wow, you said she was trying to get off the drugs. Looks like she was successful."

He shrugged and looked up to meet her eyes. "Maybe. She'd gotten clean before and gone back to it, so…"

Moved by his pain, she reached over and clasped his hand in hers. "I really am sorry."

"Anyway, I don't know what Will saw or heard that night, but until he deals with it, he's never going to get over it…or stop having nightmares."

"Poor kid."

"Yeah. Some nights are rough."

"Where were you that night?"

He grimaced. "I was with a patient at the hospital almost all night in Bryson City. I didn't find out about the fire until the next morning when the social worker brought Will to me."

He was with a patient all night. Easy enough to confirm. Her heart warmed. Her instincts were right. He didn't have anything to do with the fire. Her eyes grew heavy.

Paige reached over and squeezed his fingers. "I'm sorry, Dylan, I'm fading. Can we talk later?"

"Sure. I shouldn't have stayed so long."

She was glad he had. With a pang, she realized she didn't want him to leave. But he sure couldn't stay.

Then she couldn't hold back the yawn that hit her. Her eyelids felt like they had weights attached.

Dylan gave a small smile and glanced at his watch. "You'd better get some rest. I'm going to check in with Eli and see if he's made any headway on who trashed my office."

Paige nodded, grateful that her head only protested with a mild squeak instead of the raging scream that had accompanied that movement more than once since she'd awakened in the hospital.

With one last, lingering look that she wasn't sure how to interpret, Dylan rose and headed for the door. Paige waited at the window until he got in his car and drove off. Then she made her way back to the couch. Light-headedness hit her, and she collapsed onto the cushions.

Grabbing the light blue blanket she kept thrown over the back of the couch, she pulled it over her and let her eyes drift shut.

Her last coherent thought was that she was more certain than ever that Dylan didn't have anything to do with the fire that had killed Larry and Dylan's sister. And that was a good thing because for the first time in her career, her heart was getting way too involved.

*Thud!*

Paige jerked awake. Heart thumping, blood humming in her veins, she sat up.

The first thing she noticed was the lack of pain in her head.

The second thing that caught her attention was the fact that she'd apparently slept all day because the sun was going down just outside the window behind the couch.

The third thing made her freeze, all senses on high alert.

Someone was in her house.

Her drug-induced haze had evaporated with the sudden rush of adrenaline. She needed her gun.

But it was in her bedroom in the end table in the gun box.

Making a mental note to keep it with her from now on, she slid off the couch and her bare feet hit the carpet. Her left hand grabbed the cordless handset from the end table.

She might need it.

Paige's eyes scanned the open room, registering each detail. The family room blended into the kitchen separated by the large countertop. The breakfast area looked undisturbed. That left the two bedrooms.

One of which contained her gun.

Throat dry, breathing controlled into shallow breaths, thoughts slid through her mind as she crept on quiet feet toward her bedroom. Who would be in her house? And why? Had her cover been blown? If so, how? And where had the sound come from?

The laundry room? The only way to access that was through the breakfast area.

She just wasn't sure. And she didn't want a confrontation without her weapon. Physically, she didn't think she could handle it. Not today.

Pulse pounding doubletime, all senses tuned for another noise that didn't belong, she used the moonlight filtering through her still open blinds to guide her.

Paige passed the kitchen and paused at the door that led to the hallway. Cautiously, she peered around the edge, thankful she'd left the small night-light burning.

Nothing.

Pulling in another breath, fingers clutched around the cordless handset, she slipped through the door and into the hallway. To the right was the guest bedroom. The left, hers.

She turned left.

Stomach swirling, Paige slid the few steps to the door and again, peered inside from around the edge of the frame.

No one. Her stomach relaxed a fraction.

Moving quickly, yet still doing her best to stay quiet, she set the phone on the end table then pulled the drawer open. Inside lay the box sheltering her weapon. Paige punched in the code and the door opened with a soft pop. Curling her fingers around the butt of the gun, she flipped the safety off.

The hair on the back of her neck bristled and she spun, eyes probing the shadows of her room.

And still nothing stood out to her. Her heart pounded, adrenaline rushed. The bathroom door stood open and she could see inside. The shower curtain was still open, slid to one side, just the way she'd left it. A glance in the mirror above the sink showed no one hovering behind the door.

And yet...

Shivers danced up her spine as she assessed the

window. The closed curtains looked untouched, pulled together, also just like she'd left them.

But the bottom of one fluttered.

Paige chilled. She hadn't opened that window. But there was no place to hide, except…

Her eyes dropped to the bed.

A hand shot out, clamped around her left ankle and jerked.

# FIVE

Crashing to the floor, her elbow cracked against the hard wood sending shooting pain up to her shoulder and all through her head again.

Her gun flew from her suddenly numb fingers, and Paige knew without a doubt, in spite of her taller-than-average height and training, she was in no shape to ward off an attack.

Stunned, she lay on the floor, fighting the pain and pretending the fall had knocked her out. She gathered her wits and scrambled for a plan, as she hoped her attacker wouldn't put a bullet or a knife in her while she lay there.

Movement to her left. A subtle shift in the air around her told her whoever had been under her bed was now crawling out—on the other side.

Darting to her feet, she spun, ignoring the raging pain in her arm and the little men with jackhammers in her head. "Who are you? What do you want?" As she spoke, she moved backward, using her bare foot to feel for the gun.

Her brain registered what physical details she could see in the darkened room. About her height, wide shoulders, black mask, black clothing.

Paige felt her heart thudding in her chest and worked to control her breathing and the nausea clawing in her throat.

The figure remained silent, but she could hear his rapid, hitching breaths. Paige's foot grazed her weapon. Throwing herself to the floor, she wrapped her fingers around the butt of the gun and rolled until her back was up against the wall.

She froze, trying to listen.

Silence.

And her eyes landed on empty space.

Her intruder was gone.

She bolted after him, doubled over with pain yet determined to see as much as she could. Did he drive? Where was he parked? Before she could get out of her bedroom door, she heard her front door slam shut.

Giving chase would be futile in her condition, but she had to try. She reached the door, head and arm throbbing. Throwing it open, she held her gun ready in case he was waiting for her. She stepped out onto the porch.

Empty.

Taillights faded in the distance.

Her intruder?

Probably.

In disgust, she returned to her house and grabbed another painkiller while she punched in a number on her cell phone. Reporting it to the police would just bring more unwanted attention down on her. She wouldn't call the police, but Charles needed to know.

After another round of prayers asking for a good night's sleep, Dylan tucked Will into the bed for the fourth time and sat on the edge. "'Night, buddy."

Will reached out and squeezed Dylan's fingers. He might as well have wrapped his hand around Dylan's heart. Surprised at the gesture of affection, he tried not to let his excitement show. Instead, he smiled and leaned over to plant a kiss on the boy's forehead.

Will let his gaze linger on Dylan's face, then he turned on his side and closed his eyes.

The lump in Dylan's throat grew, and it took several swallows to get it down. How he wished he'd been a bigger part of Will's life before Sandra had died. But she hadn't let him. She'd been desperate to hide her renewed drug habit from him.

And it hadn't been hard. At first.

Dylan had been so wrapped up in Erica, first as the woman he was dating, then as his fiancée for a year, that he hadn't paid much attention to what Sandra was doing.

It wasn't until his sister had started asking for money just about every week that Dylan remembered Sandra's previous pattern. After playing private detective one weekend, he'd figured out what she was doing.

Sickened at the thought that the money he'd been giving her had gone up her nose or in her veins, he'd confronted her and threatened to turn her in to the cops.

She'd been furious. Then tearful. Then begged him not to because Will would be taken away from her.

Dylan closed his eyes as guilt swept over him.

If he'd turned her in, would she be alive today? Maybe.

When it looked like Will was going to stay in the bed this time, Dylan rose and made his way into the den. His housekeeper and part-time babysitter, Cheryl Hunt, walked from the kitchen drying her hands. The lively, sixty-year-old woman had become more like a mother to him than hired help. "Well, if you don't need me any longer, I suppose I'll be on my way."

Dylan smiled. "Thanks, Cheryl. Don't know what I'd do without you."

She waved a hand in dismissal. "Oh, you'd figure something out."

He laughed and walked her out to her car. Once again, just like in the hospital, he had that feeling of being watched. Spinning around, his eyes probed the darkness, looking for any sign of movement. His ears pricked, listening, alert.

"Dylan? Are you all right?"

He jerked. Cheryl stared at him, her forehead pinched with concern.

Helping her into the car, he reassured her. "I'm fine. Just thinking about something."

"Do you want me to stay a little longer?"

Dylan shivered as the hair on the back of his neck spiked. "No." He forced a smile. "We're good for the night. You drive safe."

He waited until she was settled in her car and pulling out of the drive before narrowing his gaze and looking around. His heart thudded as he examined the bushes lining the house.

Nothing.

Standing still, he let his eyes wander the property as his ears tuned in to the night sounds.

More nothing.

With slow, measured steps, he reentered the house, shut the door and locked it.

Taking a deep breath, he ordered his heart to slow its rapid beat.

Silence settled in on him. Around him.

Slipping to the side window, he pushed aside the curtain and looked out. The motion lights on the corners of his house only illuminated so far. Beyond them, it was pitch black.

But nothing moved.

Senses still in alert mode, he allowed his mind to drift to Paige Worth. Now there was an interesting woman. Pretty, tall enough he didn't get a crick in his neck when looking down at her, and from all indications, she had an independent streak a mile wide.

He liked that.

His eyes trailed back in the direction of Will's room. "And she obviously likes kids." Speaking the words out loud made him laugh at himself. "You've got to get a life, Seabrook."

Then he frowned. No, right now, Will was his life. Until the little boy felt comfortable and learned to trust again, Dylan would put his own life on hold.

Although Paige sure did seem to bring out the best in Will.

He wondered if she would bring out the best in *him*. He thought he might like to find out. When the time was right, of course. And if she shared his love for God.

*What do You think, Lord?*

Dylan walked to the couch and sat down, grabbing the cordless handset. He'd already memorized Paige's number, and he punched it in. It was only nine-thirty. Not too late to call.

He hung up.

Unless she was still sleeping.

But she'd probably slept all day, he argued with himself.

Redialing the number, he felt his heart pick up speed in anticipation of hearing her voice.

"Hello?"

"Hi, Paige, it's Dylan. I just called to check and see how you were feeling."

"I'm doing fine, thanks."

Something in her voice made him frown. "Are you sure?"

"Absolutely."

"You don't really sound fine."

A breathy laugh filtered through the line. "I promise, Dylan, I'm fine." A pause. "But thanks for checking on me."

"Sure." An awkward silence. Then Dylan cleared his throat. "Did you eat supper?"

"Uh…not yet."

His suspicions aroused, he asked, "Do you have any food in the house?"

Silence. "Dylan, I'm a big girl. I promise I can take care of myself."

Dylan knew he flushed even though she couldn't see him. He was kicking himself for not checking to make sure she had something to eat before he left. "Right. Sorry. I just…"

Her voice softened. "I know. Thanks, though."

He didn't want to let her off the line, but he couldn't think of anything intelligent to say. Better stop while he was ahead. "Talk to you later?"

"Sure. Bye."

For several minutes after she hung up, Dylan sat still, staring at the wall. Then a smile curved his lips, and he dialed another number.

"Hi Cheryl, it's Dylan. I was wondering if you and some of the ladies in the church would be willing to help me help a friend."

Three days later, after a clean bill of health and enough casseroles in her refrigerator to last her at least a decade, thanks to Dylan and his friends from church, Paige climbed in her car and made the short drive to the school.

The cloudy, gray sky said she'd better have an umbrella handy. Rain was in the forecast and a tornado watch had been issued. She'd forego walking until the weather cleared up.

When she'd told Charles about the intruder in her house, he'd been deeply concerned. "Are you hurt?"

"No." Well, her arm still ached, but the pain pills she'd been taking for her head had helped the arm, too.

"Is your cover blown?"

Paige had thought it over very carefully. "I

really don't think so. It could have just been a random thing. The neighborhood's not the worst in town, but it's not the best, either. Don't pull me yet. Let's see if anything else happens. I'm not ready to give up before I've even really gotten started."

"What about Dylan Seabrook? Have you gotten any vibes on whether he knows what his sister was involved with?"

Oh, she'd gotten vibes all right. But not ones she cared to share with Charles. "He figured out she was doing drugs. But I don't think he knows anything about where she was getting them."

"He's a doctor. He wasn't prescribing them for her?"

The thought had occurred to her. "I don't think so. She was more into cocaine from what I understand. But it wouldn't be a bad idea to run his license and see who he's prescribing for."

"I'll do it."

"He also has an alibi for the night of the fire." Paige gave him the information, and he promised to check it out.

Charles had called her back the next day saying Dylan had prescribed a few drugs but nothing addictive. A couple of antibiotics and a cough medicine for Will.

And he'd been at the hospital with a patient all

night. Relief flowed through her. Not that she'd really thought he had anything to do with the fire, but his nice, solid alibi made her feel better about him.

The school came into view, and she pulled into the parking lot. The rain threatened to start at any moment, so she grabbed her umbrella from the backseat.

The minute she hit the front door, the skies let loose. Paige hurried into the office, shutting the door on the deafening noise.

"Good morning, can I help you?" The woman's ID badge read Heather Wilson.

Paige stepped forward. "Hello, Ms. Wilson, I'm Paige Worth, the new guidance counselor."

The secretary's eyes went wide. "Oh! You're the one who saved little Will Price, aren't you?"

Oh, boy. Word traveled fast in a small town. Of course, the incident had taken place right outside the front door of the school. She wondered if she would encounter answering questions about saving Will all day long.

Probably. Paige forced a smile. "Yes. I just happened to be in the right place at the right time." She glanced around. "And now that I'm feeling better, I'm ready to get to work."

"Well, we're glad to have you." Paige breathed a relieved sigh when the woman let the subject of the rescue drop. Ms. Wilson grabbed a set of keys and a badge from her desk and said, "If you'll follow me, I'll show you to your office and you can get settled." She handed Paige the badge. "You'll need that to access certain areas of the building. Just swipe it with the strip facing the door."

Paige took it and clipped it on her shirt. She'd had her picture made the day of the interview. The day she'd been officially hired by the superintendent.

Ms. Wilson bustled on. "Dr. Bridges is in a meeting at the moment, but I'm sure he'll stop in to check on you later when he hears."

"Sounds great."

Paige followed the woman out of the double doors and down the hall.

Ms. Wilson unlocked the door and stepped back. "Everything should be in there. I think it's still pretty well-organized. Once you familiarize yourself with the location of everything, you shouldn't have any trouble jumping right in."

Paige looked around the office. It was a nice-size room broken into different areas. A large carpet surrounded by toys, a couch facing a rocking chair and a long conference table in front of the window. She smiled at Ms. Wilson. "This should be just fine."

The woman nodded, pulled a key off the key ring and handed it to Paige. "That will get you in the building and your office. Also, there have been tornado watches posted in recent weeks so we're going to have a tornado drill later today. Just follow the crowd and do what they do and you'll be fine."

Paige thanked her and Ms. Wilson left.

Instead of jumping in and getting to know the room, Paige decided to get to know some of the people—and see what kind of information she could glean.

She couldn't think of a better place to get started than the teacher's lounge.

As she stepped out of her office, she noticed the janitor sweeping the hallway. "Excuse me, could you tell me where the teacher's lounge is?"

His dark eyes gave her an assessing look then focused in on her badge. A friendly smile curved his lips revealing a dimple in his left cheek. "You're new, aren't you?" Paige told him who she was, and he gave her directions, then said, "I'm Sam Hobbs. If you need anything else, just let me know."

"Thanks." She headed in the direction he'd pointed. When she reached the right door, she looked back and found him still watching her, a gleam in his eye. She gave a silent snort. Well, he could forget that. She was on the job. She didn't have time for romantic entanglements.

Dylan's handsome face came immediately to mind, and she felt the heat creep into her neck.

But if she did have time, she had to admit Dylan would be the one she would be interested in. *No, you're interested in finding out what Will might know about his mother's death.*

*Focus on the job, Paige, the job, remember?*

Reaching out, she pushed the handle.

Locked.

"You need your ID for that room."

Paige turned to see the owner of the soft voice with the slight, Irish accent. A pretty, redheaded woman with brilliant green eyes smiled at her.

Paige gripped her ID. "Ah, of course. Thanks."

"I'm Fiona Whitley. I teach second grade."

They shook hands. "Paige Worth. I'm the new guidance counselor."

"Oh, lovely. We've missed having one in the school. So glad to have you here."

Paige smiled. "Thanks so much." She swiped her card and the two women entered the lounge together.

Two more staff members sat on the sofa in the corner. Another poured coffee from the glass carafe. All three turned to stare at Paige. She smiled. "Hi."

After a round of introductions and a few minutes of small talk, she decided to put the question out there. "I need someone to put a rumor to rest for me."

"What's that?" The redhead who'd introduced herself as Fiona Whitley asked.

Paige pretended to fidget. "I don't know. Maybe I shouldn't even bring it up, but it's kind of bothering me."

Of course, she had them now.

"Go ahead and ask. If there's a rumor going around that's not true, we need to know what it is so we can nip it." The blonde-headed woman who looked to be in her early thirties frowned. Jessica Stanton. Paige noted her name from the badge she had clipped to her lapel.

Paige blew out a breath and said, "All right. I... um...heard that there were drugs in this school. If that's true, I need to know which children might be most affected by this. Or if you personally know of any children whose parents are users."

"What? That's crazy!" Jessica looked offended, nostrils flaring. "Where did you hear that?"

Paige swallowed then offered a shrug. "I'm sorry. Maybe this was the wrong time and place to bring it up." Actually, it was the perfect time and place.

"No." This from the redheaded Fiona. "It's all right. If someone is saying that kind of stuff, we need to take it to the principal. And we do know of two arrests made. They were parents of two students here at the school."

The third woman in the room, Betty Lawson, a gray-haired lady who looked to be on the verge of retirement age, stepped forward and spoke. "It's not so crazy." She sighed. "My grandson is nine years old and in the fourth grade over in Bryson City. My daughter called last week to tell me he came home with a joint. Someone had put it in his backpack. They're jumping through all kinds of hoops to figure out where it came from." She shook her head. "I'm sure some of that goes on around here."

Paige listened with interest and made a mental note about the incident. She wondered if the drugs showing up in the Bryson City elementary school could be from the same source as the ones Larry had been so sure were in this school.

Something to definitely consider.

Soon, the ladies left to get back to their classes. Fiona lingered. "I really hope you can help. I wouldn't be surprised if there were drugs in this school." She frowned. "Unfortunately, drug use even in this small town seems to be on the rise."

"Really?"

"My brother is one of the deputies here in town. He and all of our law enforcement here have been busier than ever before trying to crack down on the drugs." She shook her head, her eyes sad. "I hate it, but what else do you do other than fight it?"

Paige could tell it bothered the woman. Just as she was about to ask about Sandra, Dylan's sister, the door opened and Dylan popped his head in.

"Hey, there, ladies."

When her heart thudded a happy beat, she took note of the reaction and told herself to cool it. She was on the job.

Her heart didn't care. "Hi, what are you doing here? Is Will okay?"

A warm light from his eyes smiled at her before his lips curved. "Will is fine. Sometimes I fill in as the school nurse when she's out sick." He flashed his school badge at her.

Fiona cleared her throat, and Paige gave a slight start. Had she actually forgotten the woman was there? She felt a flush creep up her neck. Fiona's eyes twinkled as they darted back and forth between her and Dylan. Then she smiled as though she had a secret. "Hello, Dylan."

"Hi, Fiona."

"It's been a while since you have been over for supper. Do you think you and Will can make one night this week?"

Paige thought Dylan's cheeks looked a little ruddier than usual as he looked at the woman who was obviously more than a coworker. A spurt of jealousy shot through her, and she blinked.

Dylan nodded. "Possibly. If Joseph can stop playing with the horses long enough."

A laugh escaped Fiona's throat. She said to Paige. "Joseph's my husband. We own one of the horse farms up on the mountain."

Husband. Fiona was married. Relief nearly melted her knees.

Fiona looked at Paige, then cut her eyes to Dylan. "Feel free to bring a guest if you want."

Before Dylan could respond, Fiona glanced at her watch and headed for the door. "Oh! Gotta run. Very nice to meet you, Paige." To Dylan she said, "See you soon."

When she left, silence reigned for an awkward moment. Then Paige said, "That's really nice of you to offer your time here at the school when they need you." In fact, he'd been nothing but nice since she'd met him.

He waved aside her praise but she couldn't help notice the tinge of red in his cheeks still hadn't disappeared. "It's hard to find a substitute nurse in this little town. When the principal, Tom, brought his daughter in one day last year for a checkup, he asked almost as a joke if I knew anyone who might want the extra hours working as a sub for the school nurse. I said I'd do it if I could rearrange my patients for the day. Today I could."

She flashed him a knowing look. "And you don't mind seeing Will throughout the day, either, do you?"

He shot her that perfect smile, and her lungs forgot how to work. "There is that," he agreed. His eyes lowered, then raised to meet hers again. "Do you have plans for supper tonight?"

Was he asking her out? What would she say if he was? *Yes,* her heart demanded, *say yes.* The professional side of her wanted to argue. She compromised. "I'll probably heat up another one of those delicious casseroles taking up space in my freezer."

His eyes twinkled. "How about pizza instead?"

"Hmm." She tapped her lip and pretended to think about it. "How about you and Will come over and help me empty my freezer. It's your fault I have way too much food."

"My fault?" His innocent look didn't fool her. A pang of guilt hit her. She definitely wanted to spend the time with him tonight, but had to admit she was hoping she could get some more information from him—and see if Will would talk to her.

"Yes." She shoved the guilt aside and smiled. "And I appreciated it very much. So—" she rubbed her hands together "—tonight?"

The door opened and two staff members entered, stopping when they spotted Paige and Dylan. Paige smiled then looked at Dylan. "Five?"

"See you then."

Dylan left.

After more introductions, Paige took the opportunity to do a little more fishing.

She filled a foam cup full of the ever-available coffee and took a seat on the sofa.

A dark-headed woman who introduced herself as Leslie sat opposite Paige. "Where are you from?"

And so the small talk went.

Paige finally was able to bring the conversation around to Sandra Price. "Did any of you know her?"

"She subbed here a few times. Seemed like a nice enough person."

Paige caught the hesitation in the woman's voice. "But?"

"I heard she was pretty messed up. Drugs."

"Really?"

"Yes, but Dr. Seabrook did a lot for her and Will, I think. I overheard her talking about how fortunate she was to be able to count on her brother for help when she needed it." She shrugged. "Jessica Stanton would know more. She was pretty good friends with Sandra, even taking care of Will some on the weekends."

Making a mental note to question Jessica further about how well she knew Sandra, Paige glanced at the clock. She had one more thing to take care of.

Excusing herself, she went to find Dylan again. In her happiness at seeing him—and the brain fog she seemed to get every time he flashed that smile at her—she forgot to ask him if he'd made any progress on finding names of patients who might hold a grudge against him. On the way to his office, she worked on a way to ask him that wouldn't sound as if she was a cop.

Frustration bit at her. She liked Dylan—a lot. And she found herself wanting to be honest with him. But she couldn't risk that yet.

Larry had been honest with Sandra, and that may have been part of the reason he'd been killed.

No, while she didn't believe he had anything to do with the fire that killed Larry and Sandra, she still wasn't ready to put her life in Dylan's hands.

# SIX

Dylan bandaged the elbow of the overenthusiastic, eight-year-old, indoor kick ball champion and sent the girl on her way with a pass. As the child headed back to class, he sat down to write his short note in the log and then one explaining the incident to the parent.

He checked his to-do list.

Reference for Kyle. Check. Printed, signed and delivered.

Call Margaret for an update on Dr. Bailey and if he'd shown up for work today. He had. And seemed to be having a good day.

*Thank you, Lord. He needs Your healing.* Check.

A knock on the door interrupted him. Looking up, he saw Paige slip inside.

Keep heart in chest and don't say anything dumb. Check. Hopefully. "Hey, again," he said. Yep, she looked as good as she did fifteen minutes ago in the lounge.

"I was just thinking about you. Earlier, I forgot

to ask if you'd figured out who ransacked your office. Any patients with grudges turn up?"

Dylan lifted a brow then shrugged. "I've been thinking about it. Going through past cases, but I've not really come up with anything, nor have the police."

"What about when you were a resident?"

"Well, nothing comes to mind there, either. And I wouldn't have access to those files now, anyway." He cocked his head and studied her. "Why so full of questions this morning?"

She stood in the doorway, bottom lip tucked up under her front teeth as she thought. He smiled. She almost looked like a little girl deep in concentration.

When she looked up, her gaze collided with his. Nope, she was all woman.

"Like I said, I was just wondering. Thinking about it. About you. In fact, I'd be happy to help you go through the files if you like. We could make the list for the sheriff and let him take it from there."

His heart warmed. She'd been thinking about him and his problems. Her offer to help made his pulse jump.

Paige placed a hand on the door to leave, and he stopped her with, "We'll see about the files. Thanks for the offer. And five tonight, right?"

A flush heated her cheeks. "Five o'clock." With one last smile, she left.

He glanced at his watch. Seven hours until he would see her again. Dylan decided time had just slowed to a practical standstill.

Paige left the nurse's office and knew her face was beet-red. Deciding it would do no good to berate herself for giving in to the desire to see Dylan, and using the excuse of checking to see if he'd made progress on his search through his files, she went back to her office and started making out a schedule.

For the first few days, she would be excused from seeing children as she settled into her room, waded through the stack of referrals and contacted teachers. At least that's what she would give the appearance of doing. Hopefully, by the time she was expected to start seeing children, she would have this case wrapped up.

However, if she didn't, she wasn't too concerned. One of her areas of interest had been studying the effects of crime on children and the best kinds of therapy to help them cope.

One of the reasons she'd chosen the guidance counselor cover. She wouldn't be stuck in a classroom all day and could come and go as she needed to.

If it came down to it, she would follow the curriculum and do some simple lessons on various topics like the evils of drugs and alcohol, domestic violence and bullying.

But mostly, she'd cover drugs and see if she got any response from the children. If there were drugs in this school, and Larry had thought there were, then someone knew something. Most likely, one of the children.

She'd just have to be very careful about how she gathered her information. And if she came across an issue that she felt needed more than what she could offer, she would make a referral to another professional.

The feeling of being watched made her swirl around in her chair.

The hair on the back of her neck spiked.

No one. Her door stood open.

Noise from the hallway reached her.

Getting up, she crossed the room to look out.

Nothing to the left.

When she looked right, her gaze landed on little Will Price. Her pulse slowed. He stood, somber, his blue eyes probing.

She smiled and dropped to her knees to look him in the eye. "Hello, Will. How are you today?"

His tongue darted to lick his lips.

Her gaze sharpened. Did he want to tell her something? "Do you want to come in my office?"

Will looked behind him, so Paige asked. "Where's your class?"

Still nothing—but his mouth opened, then shut.

Paige pushed one more time. "Do you want to come in, honey?"

He took a step toward her, mouth open as though to speak.

A teacher rounded the corner and stopped when she saw Will and Paige in the hallway. Forcing a smile, the woman said, "There you are, Will. I've been looking for you. You're not supposed to wander off like that."

Will snapped his lips shut, turned from Paige and obediently walked to his teacher's side. But when he turned back for one more lingering look at Paige, she couldn't help but wonder if he'd been about to say something.

Regret pierced her. She would have to make time to call Will down to her office and do a little play-therapy with him. Maybe once he decided he trusted her more, he would open up.

Then again, he seemed to trust Dylan and didn't utter a word to the man who so obviously loved him.

Sighing, she went back into the office to finish the schedule and do her best to pretend she wasn't excited about seeing Dylan and Will tonight.

At four o'clock, Paige finally noticed the silence in the building. Elementary schools shut down pretty quick in the afternoon. Closing her planner, she rose from the desk and grabbed her keys. She wanted to get home and grab a shower before her company arrived.

Movement near her door caught her attention, and she stopped, waiting for the person to enter. Tom Bridges stepped inside and smiled. "I'm sorry I didn't get by earlier. How was your first day?"

Paige relaxed. "Just fine, thanks. You have very friendly staff here."

"And we're delighted you joined us. Melanie, our previous counselor, was wonderful, but she decided to stay home with her baby instead of coming back, so we've been rather stuck. The middle school counselor has been pulling double duty for a while now." After inquiring into her well-being, he glanced at his watch. "But I think you've put in a full day and it's time to head out. You don't want to overdo it."

"I was just leaving," she said as she gathered her belongings.

He had his keys in his hand. "I'm parked on the other side of the building, so I'm going out the back door. See you tomorrow."

"Dr. Bridges, do you mind if I ask you a quick question?"

He lifted a brow. "Sure."

Paige sighed. "I know today is only my first

day, and I hate to stir up anything that I shouldn't, but I've heard some rumors and thought I'd ask you about them."

Dr. Bridges nodded. "The parents arrested for drugs?"

"Yes."

He shook his head. "It's a sad situation. The children are no longer in the school. They've been taken by DSS and placed with other family members. One in Bryson City and one in Asheville."

"I see." She paused. "Do you suspect any other parents who might be involved?"

Frowning, he said, "I can't think of anyone. The two arrested were good friends. Roommates, I believe." He studied her. "Eli, our sheriff, has already investigated the situation."

Paige forced a smile. "I'm sure. I just wanted to be on top of everything in case I came across a child in a similar environment."

His shoulders relaxed a fraction. "Well, that's not a bad idea. Thanks for making me aware of your concerns. If I come up with anything new or think you need to focus on any particular child, I'll let you know."

"That'd be great."

He left and Paige shifted the bag over her shoulder as she walked out the front door. Thankfully, the rain had stopped, although the sky promised more was on the way.

On the way to her car, she noticed Sam Hobbs, the janitor, emptying a trash can into a larger bin. He nodded as she walked past. "Have a good afternoon, ma'am."

"You, too, Mr. Hobbs."

He smiled. "Sam."

"Bye, Sam."

Then she stopped. Of all the people in the school, maybe he was the one she needed to talk to. Quickly coming up with a story, Paige turned back. "Sam, in the curriculum I have to use with the kids, I'll be talking about drug use. One of the teachers mentioned her grandson came home with drugs in his backpack but claims he doesn't know how they got there. You're all over this school. Have you ever heard of anything like that happening here?"

His brows furrowed as he thought. "No, not here. I mean, out of all the kids that go here, I wouldn't doubt a few of the parents have done drugs at some point, but I haven't personally seen anything."

"Hmm. Well, thanks." She should have figured. Even if he knew something, he might hesitate saying anything to the new person. Understandable. What she didn't get was the fact that the drug dogs hadn't come up with anything tangible.

"Sure thing. See you tomorrow."

From what she'd read in the report, after the

arrest of the two parents, a drug dog had been brought in. The dog had alerted to a few of the kids' backpacks, but that could be because their parents smoked marijuana at home, or it could be the child was at a friend's house and someone in that house smoked it.

But nothing had turned up.

The fact was, unless the drugs were found at the time of the alerting by the dog, there wasn't much she or anyone else could do about it.

Paige continued on to her car, anxious to get home and get ready for the evening ahead. Although the skies still threatened, she was grateful that the rain had stopped for now. Tossing her unopened umbrella in the backseat, she climbed in and turned the key.

Nothing. Not even a click.

What?

She tried again.

Still nothing.

"Great." She slapped the wheel. Not now. A glance at her watch showed it was already 4:23.

Reaching under the dash, Paige popped the hood. Climbing out of the vehicle, she exposed the engine and gaped.

Her battery was gone.

Paige's blood pressure spiked. Spinning on her heel, she looked around the parking lot.

No one in sight.

Even Tom Bridges's car was gone.

A red truck sat in a parking spot about six spaces down. Probably belonged to Sam Hobbs. But what could he do? She needed a battery.

Then again, he'd been outside emptying trash. The bins were to her right within line of sight of her car. He may have seen something, someone tampering with her vehicle. Sam'd already disappeared into the building.

Now she stood alone in the parking lot.

Alone.

Her mind clicked.

Okay, go question Sam or figure out what this meant.

Someone wanted her to be here. Someone wanted her stranded, unable to leave.

Taking her battery shouted that real clear.

But who? And why? And *where* was the person who'd snatched her battery?

Close by and watching?

Watching for what?

For her to start walking home?

A quick look at the street showed it was busy, cars passing in front of the school on a regular basis.

But people had disappeared on busy streets before.

Paige looked at the lock on the door. She knew for a fact she'd locked it when she climbed out that morning, but someone skilled with a coat hanger or access to a professional locksmith tool could easily gain entry without leaving a clue behind.

Reaching into the backseat, she pulled out her purse, set it on the hood of her car and dug out her cell phone.

Wheels crunched on the asphalt behind her. Whirling, her hand went to her shoulder holster— the one that wasn't there. Blood still pumping, she moved so that her car was between her and the vehicle that pulled up beside her.

Simon Moore. The reporter. A small grin pulled at his lips as he lowered the driver's side window. "Trouble?"

Paige straightened. "Someone stole my battery. You wouldn't happen to know who, would you?"

A hurt look crossed his face. "Well, thanks a lot."

She grimaced. "Sorry. I'm in a bad mood." Even though she had her suspicions, she supposed she should get proof before making accusations. Paige gestured to the car. "This wasn't exactly what I wanted to come out and find. What are you doing here, anyway?" she asked.

"Looking for you."

"Well, you found me." *And I'm still not talking,* she thought, hoping he could read her face. "Why are you being so persistent?"

"Why are you being so secretive?"

"Secretive?" Was that how she came across? "Not to be rude, but maybe I just don't like reporters."

"Look, I'm just trying to do my job." He snorted. "My goal is not to stay in this rinky-dink town for the rest of my life. I need a story to give me the edge over my competitors. Is that so wrong?"

Without hesitation, she said, "It is when you go about it the way you are." Narrowing her eyes, she stared at him. "Did you steal my battery?"

Moore rolled his eyes. "Can I give you a ride or not?"

Paige bit her lip and looked at her car. Then back at the reporter.

She supposed she didn't have a choice unless she wanted to walk—a raindrop splashed on her cheek—and get wet.

"Let me see some ID," she said.

Moore's left brow shot north. "Why? You don't believe me?"

Paige kept silent and just stared. Anyone could spin a good I-just-want-out-of-this-small-town story if he practiced it enough.

With another impatient roll of his eyes, Moore complied by flashing his newspaper-employee badge.

Satisfied, she nodded. "Fine. Let me just get my stuff."

Another vehicle turned into the parking lot, and Paige breathed a glad sigh when she saw it was Dylan and Will.

He pulled up beside her and the reporter. Eyes darting between them, he rolled down the window. "Can I help?"

From the backseat, Will watched the adults. Thankfully, he didn't look scared, just curious.

Paige nodded. "Can you give me a ride to my house? Someone stole my car battery."

With an eye on the reporter, Dylan nodded. "Hop in."

"Oh, come on," Moore protested. "I just want to talk." His gaze zeroed in on Will. "Hey, is that the kid? Will he tell me about—"

"No," Dylan interrupted, fury erupting on his face. "He won't."

Paige hurried around to the passenger side of Dylan's car and climbed in. Through Dylan's still-open window, she called to the reporter, "Thanks, anyway."

His eyes narrowed on her, and his lips tightened into a thin line. "See you around, Ms. Worth."

Dylan rolled up his window and headed out of the parking lot while Paige pondered Simon Moore's words. Somehow, they didn't sound like a nice parting comment. The more she thought about it, the more she decided they might be considered a threat.

Peering into the rearview mirror, she could see the man still standing beside his car, talking into a cell phone.

Had he been the one to steal her battery?

If not…then who? And why?

Dylan glanced out of the corner of his eye at the woman beside him. Deep in thought, her brow furrowed as she chewed on her bottom lip. "I'm glad I happened to pass the parking lot. Are you all right? You think that reporter stole your battery?"

She jerked and stared at him. "Yes, I'm okay. Something's just not right. First the car that nearly ran down—" She stopped and glanced in the rearview mirror.

"It's all right. He's got his earphones on. He's listening to a book on my iPod."

"—then someone breaks in my house and now this," she finished.

Dylan's fingers clenched the wheel. "Broke into your house!"

Paige blinked at him and snapped her lips together. She blew out a breath and nodded. "Yes. The night I came home from the hospital. Someone broke in. He…ran off when he realized I was awake."

Dylan pulled into her driveway and turned the engine off. "Did you call the police?"

"I reported it."

Climbing out of the car, Paige walked ahead of him to open the door to her home. Dylan got Will out and followed her inside.

"Come on in and get comfortable," she said. "Will is welcome to watch the Cartoon Channel."

"He's got his Nintendo DS game if he gets bored."

"Great. Then I'll just throw a couple of these casseroles in the oven to heat. Do you have a preference? Mexican or chicken?"

Dylan led Will into the den as he watched Paige scurry around the kitchen. "Mexican sounds good."

"Mexican it is."

He smiled when he saw her shoes tossed in the hall in front of the closet. He wondered if she'd trip over them again and give him another chance to catch her, hold her in his arms.

But Will was here. His wide eyes took in the small living area.

Dylan looked at her mantel over the fireplace, the television against the wall, the picture behind the recliner, and realized something. She had nothing personal sitting out. No family pictures.

No plants. Nothing to indicate that she planned to stay here permanently.

He also realized he knew very little about Paige's background. Every time they'd chatted, he'd done most of the talking—at least about personal stuff.

Watching her puttering around the kitchen, seeing Will relax on the sofa, his Nintendo game making soft beeping noises, made Dylan's heart stutter.

And long for a family.

Dylan walked over and picked up Paige's shoes. "Hey, where do you keep your shoes? I'll put these away for you. The hall closet?"

Her voice came from the kitchen. "Yes, thanks."

Dylan reached for the knob and tugged it open. He stopped and stared in confusion at the contents. Hurried footsteps came toward him.

"No, wait! I don't want them in…"

He heard her voice trail off as she realized what he was staring at. He turned and asked, "Why do you have a shoulder holster hanging in your closet?" He paused. "And a badge that says Paige Ashworth—DEA?"

Paige bit back the groan that threatened to escape.

Did she lie or shoot straight with him?

"I, um, I told you I had a fascination with police shows. Well, as a joke, my...brother..." She broke off, unable to look him in the eye and lie. She simply couldn't do it. If it had been anyone else, she wouldn't have batted a lash. But Dylan was different.

And yet he wasn't. She still had to find out what he knew about his sister's death. And she could see that if he thought she was lying, he'd shut her out completely.

Blowing a breath from her pursed lips, she glanced at the occupied child and said in a low voice, "I can't lie to you." She walked to the kitchen then back. "I'm DEA. I'm undercover. My real name is Ashworth."

His flinch stung her. The narrowed eyes nearly cut her in two. She lifted her chin and stared at him.

"DEA? As in Drug Enforcement Agency?" he sputtered the words.

"Yes."

Taking a step toward her, still holding her shoes, he asked, "And what's in Rose Mountain that has the DEA sending an agent out here to do undercover work?"

Paige bit her lip, uncertainty squirming inside her stomach. Then she pulled in a calming breath. "Because your sister's boyfriend, Larry Bolin, was also an undercover agent who got killed, and a lot of people want to know why—including his family."

"Family?" Dylan stilled. "Was he married?"

"No. But he was close to his parents and three brothers."

"And he was DEA."

It wasn't a question, so she didn't bother answering.

Dylan looked like he'd just received a punch to the kidney. "Sandra's boyfriend? My sister's boyfriend worked for the DEA? Did she know this?"

"Yes. He talked her into giving him as much information as possible before they died. At least that's what he told us." Compassion softened her eyes. "She was turning her life around."

"How did I not know this?"

"Eli, your sheriff, asked the DEA for help after the two parents from the elementary school were arrested. They're not talking because they're scared to death of repercussions from whoever they were getting the drugs from." Paige took the shoes from his slack fingers and placed a hand on his arm. "Why don't you sit down?"

He moved to the kitchen table and slid onto one of the chairs. His gaze darted to the den area where Will was still engrossed in his game. The timer dinged, indicating the casserole was finished.

Inhaling, she drew comfort from the delicious-smelling dish. Moving on autopilot, she dropped the shoes into the closet. Back in the kitchen, she removed the food from the oven and started pulling down plates and glasses.

Setting the table, she worked around Dylan who still seemed to be taking it all in.

"So you're here to work on the case," he said.

"Yes. But even though Eli was the one who requested the help, he doesn't yet know it's here."

He raised his eyes to meet hers. "And all those questions about what I knew about the fire. You were pumping me for information."

She blew out a deep sigh and set the silverware on the table. "Yes." She wouldn't make any excuses.

"I don't know whether to be angry or..." His voice trailed off, and Paige felt his confusion to the depths of her soul.

"I'm sorry I couldn't tell you when we first met. I had to make sure you weren't involved."

He frowned. "And you're sure now?"

She felt the flush creep up into her cheeks. "Yes. In the short time that we've known each other, I just..." She shrugged. "Call it instinct. I don't think you had anything to do with the fire or anyone's death. And your rock-solid alibi doesn't hurt, either." She tried a smile.

His shoulders relaxed a fraction. "Well, thanks for that, anyway."

"However, you can't tell anyone what I'm doing."

Dylan shook his head. "I won't say anything. I want to know who started that fire as much as anyone else. More so. Sandra didn't deserve to die like that."

"And neither did Larry." She set the food on the table and placed a serving spoon in the bowl. "You want to get Will?"

Dylan called the little boy into the kitchen, and the three of them sat down to eat. She dipped the spoon and started serving. Will simply looked at his plate, then his uncle. "Doesn't he like Mexican food?" Paige asked.

"Yes, he's, uh…waiting for us to say the blessing."

Paige swallowed, felt the heat in her cheeks. "Oh. Right. Sorry."

"It's fine." Dylan smiled at her, and she gulped at the sweet feelings running through her. He asked, "Would you like me to say it?"

"Yes, please." It had been quite a while since she'd prayed, and she wasn't sure if she even remembered how. Except to beg for help when she was in trouble.

They bowed their heads, and Dylan offered a short and very sweet prayer thanking God for everything and asking his blessing on the food. As soon as he said amen, Will picked up his fork and dug in.

Paige forgot her discomfort and laughed as she watched him eat. "I guess you were hungry, huh, kiddo?"

Will glanced at her, then went back to his food, but not before she caught the twinkle in his eye. Her heart warmed as she took in the sight of them at her table. Like a family.

Then grief pierced her.

They were the family she'd always wanted but would never have.

Gulping her water, she pushed aside the momentary crack in her usually unflappable armor.

"I'll be glad to take you to the auto-parts store downtown so you can get a battery for your car," Dylan offered.

"That's all right. I'll get it taken care of tomorrow."

He frowned at her. Paige thought he might insist, but he didn't.

Instead, he said, "So, tell me something about yourself, Paige. Something that doesn't have anything to do with what you're working on."

She lifted a brow. "What do you want to know?"

"What was your childhood like?"

Paige grimaced. The one topic she'd rather not discuss. She looked at him.

While he waited for her to answer, he took another bite of the casserole. "Well?"

Paige glanced at Will. "Probably a bit like his."

Dylan blanched. "Oh. Sorry."

She shrugged. "I've come a long way since then. I don't think about it too much anymore."

"So you still have contact with your parents?"

"My mother, not parents. I don't know who my father is. And no, I don't keep up with her anymore." Sadness filled her. Suddenly she wasn't hungry. Setting her fork down, she stood. "Anyone need anything else to drink?"

Will held his cup up to her, and she filled it with the milk she'd bought the day before. His eyes lingered on hers and she smiled. "You're welcome."

"You'll be a great mom one day," Dylan observed.

Paige froze. Then she pulled in a deep breath. "No. No, I won't. I won't ever be a mother." Her mind went back to that room where her mother's friends slept on the floor. To a little boy whose mother left him there. She remembered his coughing and how her mother ignored him through the closed door. Paige had also ignored him, replicating her mother's parenting. She willed herself to stop the flood of memories.

Dylan flinched and actually went pale. Before Paige could gather her thoughts and ask him what was wrong, a loud crash from the den jolted her to her feet.

# SEVEN

Dylan bolted after Paige, then froze, turned back to Will and saw the boy's wide, frightened eyes locked on him. Forcing a smile, Dylan went to him. But his gaze went to the woman on the other side of the kitchen counter investigating the broken window behind the couch.

"Paige, is everything all right?"

"I think so," she called back. But her voice was tight, and Dylan could tell she'd answered the way she had in order not to scare Will. She went to the hall closet. The one where he'd found her shoulder holster. Pulling out a metal box from the top shelf, she set it on the counter, then dialed the combination. Popping the top, she grabbed the contents.

He saw the glint of metal before she hid it behind her back. A gun.

A chill swept through him. "Paige?"

She shot a glance over her shoulder. "Everything's fine. I'm just going to take a look outside, all right? You stay here with Will."

Frustration hit him. "You can't go out there by yourself. What if—"

"Dylan, please. I'll be fine. I'm trained for this kind of thing, remember?"

"Then I'm calling 911. You need some backup."

"No." Her sharp tone cut into him. "I don't need that kind of attention. If I think I need backup, I'll call it in. Just stay with Will and let me do my job."

He said nothing else as she eased out the back door.

Paige's stomach twisted into knots as she looked up and down the street. Even though it was nearing six-fifteen, the sun still shone, and she could see clearly in every direction.

What had broken the window? More specifically, *who* was responsible?

Once again, she wondered if her cover had been blown. A shadow moved to her right. Her fingers gripped her gun, and she spun to see a figure dart from behind her bushes and head for a car parked across the street about three houses down.

"Freeze!" she called.

The fleeing man stopped for a brief moment but never looked back. He picked up speed once again. Paige started after him, then stopped. She could take him down, but that really would expose the fact that she wasn't who she was pretending to be.

And yet, she desperately wanted to know who this guy was. Her would-be intruder was already in the driver's seat with the engine started. Paige put on a burst of speed and got close enough to get a few digits from the license plate. "ALC 14… something," she muttered out loud.

As she reentered the house, Dylan waited for her, cordless phone in his left hand. Will sat on the couch watching a video.

She stopped. "Please tell me you didn't call anyone."

He narrowed his eyes. "I called Eli."

"The sheriff?" she nearly squeaked.

"Sorry, but there was no way I was letting you go after someone who could have a weapon or something without some kind of backup." He glanced at his nephew. "I couldn't leave him to help, so I did the only thing I could."

Unable to fathom what this might mean to her cover, she stomped to the kitchen, racking her brain for some kind of story to tell the sheriff.

Flashing red lights outside the kitchen window told her she'd better think fast.

To Dylan, she said, "Let me handle this, all right?"

"You can trust Eli."

"Right now, I can't trust anyone."

"You trusted me."

Her heart thumped. Yes, she had. And it went against everything in her to do it, because while she couldn't explain it, she knew she had to. "And you're the only one, all right?"

And then Eli was pounding on the door. "Dylan, you in there?"

Hiding her gun back in the closet, Paige opened the door and let the sheriff in. His alert, green eyes said he wasn't missing a thing and she'd better tread carefully in order not to give herself away. "What's going on here? Dylan called and said you had some kind of intruder?"

Paige let him in. "Yes. We were eating supper and heard the window in the den break. I looked outside but didn't see anything except someone running away."

Eli turned and exited the house once again. Shooting Dylan a look, she followed. Dylan's gaze went to Will. The boy was still engrossed in watching the program, so Paige wasn't surprised when Dylan turned to follow her.

The three made their way around to the broken window. "There." She crept forward, doing her best not to disturb the ground anymore than she had to. "Footprints."

"And an overturned bucket."

Dylan leaned in. "That looks like blood on that jagged piece of glass."

Eli cleared his throat. "All right, people, clearly someone was here." His eyes landed on Paige. "I'm putting this puzzle together, and I'm not liking the picture I'm getting."

Raising her brows, she blinked at him, going for her best innocent look. "What do you mean?"

"Look, first that deal with Will and the runaway car, then the break-in at Dylan's office. Now this." His astute eyes bored into her. "What's going on?"

Paige blew out a breath. This whole case was falling apart. Never in her career with law enforcement had a case gone so wrong. But she had to play it cool. Until her supervisor gave her permission to break cover—again—she had to keep a lid on it. The fact that Dylan knew would stick in Charles's craw. If she told Eli, she would jeopardize her career.

Turning, she shrugged. "I don't know. I still think Dylan must have made someone mad, and they're out to get him. I mean, that's the most logical explanation, right?"

Dylan made a choking sound in his throat, and it was all she could do not to glare at him.

Eli's gaze flicked between the two of them, then he shook his head. "Fine. Keep your secrets." He narrowed his eyes. "For now."

Dylan sighed and Paige breathed a sigh of relief. "So, what about the window? Can't you do some sort of DNA test like they do on TV and figure out who tried to break in?"

Eli's sharp gaze never wavered, and Paige couldn't tell if he was buying into her story. Finally, he looked at the window. "All right. I've got a forensics kit in the car. I'll get this blood sample to the lab." Eli left to get the equipment from his car, and Paige looked at Dylan.

"Thank you for not saying anything."

His eyes narrowed. "I still think you're wrong in not trusting Eli, but I'll respect your opinion."

"I appreciate that."

Then Eli was back.

He took the blood sample from the glass, then dusted the rest of the window.

Finally, he looked up. "There aren't any prints on here."

Paige rubbed her nose. "I'm sure the Jacksons had them cleaned before I moved in. So whoever was out there was either wearing gloves or was just looking in."

Skepticism crossed Eli's face. "Then why break the window?"

She shrugged. "I have no idea. It's probably all a coincidence."

More skepticism stamped on his features, Eli slapped his hat on his head. "When y'all are ready to come clean about what's going on, I'll be around." He held up the evidence bag. "In the meantime, I'll get this to the lab in Asheville. Don't know how long we're looking at until we get results. If the guy's not in the system, then it's not going to help us much."

"But you'll have it if you catch the person."

Shrewd eyes studied her once again. "Right."

As Eli drove away, Dylan cleared his throat. "You need to consider that your cover is blown."

Anxiety hit her. "I know. I'll think about it." And she would. But she wasn't ready to go anywhere yet. She needed to find Larry's killer. And the two people in her house were the ones that could help her do that. A little voice inside her mocked her, saying that wasn't the only reason she didn't want to concede defeat and go back to Atlanta.

She finally let herself admit she didn't want to leave Dylan and Will. She'd gotten personally involved, and the stakes were too high to quit now.

Dylan watched her come back into the house. His brain felt like it was on overload. First he'd found out she was DEA and then she announced she'd never be a mother.

A sick feeling engulfed him. Had he started falling for another woman like Erica?

Paige grabbed the blanket from the back of the couch and spread it over Will. The little boy frowned and mumbled something in his sleep.

Paige soothed the wrinkles from his forehead and stroked his hair until he settled.

Dylan watched it all with a feeling of disbelief. She was a natural, with maternal instincts she couldn't deny.

Maybe he'd misunderstood what she meant.

Paige left Will alone and paced to the window.

He motioned to the recliner. "Why don't you sit down?" He really wanted to talk to her about the things he'd just learned. She wasn't who he thought she was. The fact that he'd been falling for her concerned him.

"I feel like we need to start over," he told her.

She ignored his invitation to sit. Instead, she moved to the other window, peeled aside the edge of the curtain and looked out.

"I can't sit down. I still have adrenaline shooting through me." She shot him a glance. "What do you mean we need to start over?"

"You're not the woman I thought you were. I mean I know we haven't really known each other very long, but I was starting to get to know you, to…to hope…" he let his words trail off. He wasn't used to being vulnerable, to putting his heart on the line. After Erica's betrayal, he'd sworn off relationships—at least for the time being.

And then he'd met Paige.

Regret clouded her eyes. "I'm sorry Dylan. I didn't mean to lead you on. And while I might have feelings of guilt for some of the things I do, it's still my job. I knew what I was getting into when I chose this career so I deal with it."

"How?"

After peering outside for a long time, she responded. "Sometimes, it's harder than others," she admitted. "But I tell myself that the end justifies the means. That I'm putting criminals, murderers, drug traffickers and other really rotten people behind bars. And that's a good thing. If I have to play a role to do that, then so be it. And…sometimes I pray about it."

Hope leaped inside him. "You believe in God?"

"Yes. I believe in Him."

"I hear reservations in your voice."

With a sigh, she leaned her forehead against the wall next to the window. "It's a really long story. I don't think I want to bore you with it tonight."

Somehow, he doubted *boredom* was the right word. "Tomorrow's Saturday. Will you spend the day with Will and me?"

She paused and he could almost see her processing the invitation. Would she say no?

Did he really want her to say yes? He should be angry with her for lying to him but couldn't hold on to that feeling. And he didn't really want to. However, he did want to see her with Will to see if she could break through the silence no one else could penetrate.

Finally, she looked at him and smiled. "Sure."

Relief flooded him. "Good. Because I have some questions I need answers to."

# EIGHT

Paige watched as Dylan and Will backed out of her driveway, her eyes scanning the darkness beyond. Nothing caught her attention, but she still felt on edge, wary and watchful.

She'd enjoyed the evening for the most part—with the exception of the broken window that he'd helped her board up with some plywood she found in the garage. However, Dylan and Will's company drove home the extent of her loneliness, and she wondered if she'd ever put it behind her.

And part of her worried about Dylan knowing her true reason for being in Rose Mountain. She hoped he could handle it, that he wouldn't feel obligated to go to his friend, sheriff Eli.

She'd just have to count on his integrity. The fact that if he felt like he couldn't keep her secret, he would at least give her a heads-up that he planned to tell Eli.

Paige pulled on a pair of black gloves.

Her plan tonight was to get to the school and

get inside to do some snooping. Thanks to the superintendent, she had the alarm code.

Ten minutes later, dressed in black and armed with her weapon, she threw on a raincoat and stuffed a black hat into the pocket. Hoping she looked like any other normal person out for an evening walk, she headed down the street to the school. It was only a five-minute bike ride. Walking would take her a bit longer.

The rain had stopped, but the humidity hung heavy in the air. Before too long, she was drenched with sweat. Ignoring it, she kept to the sidewalk, taking note of the occasional car that passed by. In the small town of Rose Mountain, no doubt someone would mention her late-night stroll. She already had her cover story, though.

She'd simply say she forgot something in her car and went to get it.

That was one reason she hadn't let Dylan get her a battery. She'd already been planning this little trek while she'd been serving the casserole.

Her phone vibrated.

Pulling it out, she saw she had a text message. From Dylan. Pressing the appropriate button, she read, I called Buddy at the auto store. He went by and put a battery in your car.

Paige nearly stumbled. "You did what?" she asked aloud. She was stunned, surprised. Touched. Dylan had gone out of his way to do something very thoughtful for her. When was the last time someone had done something like that just to make things easier on her?

Paige's heart throbbed when she realized she honestly couldn't remember. Being such a loner and so engrossed in her job didn't make it easy to cultivate long-term friendships. Sure, she had her buddies at the office and her boss, Charles, was a good man who treated her well, but... It wasn't the same. That was work. She could admit she wanted more.

She decided she liked the good doctor quite a bit more each time she saw him or had contact with him.

Amazingly enough, she also decided she liked the feeling of being cared for—of someone looking out for her and doing those kinds of things for her, like putting a battery in her car.

Yeah, she liked it a lot. Paige felt a smile curve her lips as she texted back. Thanks. Now I owe you more than a frozen casserole.

Guilt stabbed her. Everyone she'd met in this town, from Dylan to the people at the school, had gone out of their way to make her feel welcome. None of that small-town hostility toward newcomers that could be found in some places. Rose Mountain had good folks. Deceiving them stung.

But it was her job. And taking drug dealers and

their product off the street was doing what was best for the town in the long run.

She'd accept their kindness and hopefully repay it by doing her job the best way she knew how.

Thankfully, she'd grabbed her car keys before leaving the house. She could drive home when she was finished at the school.

Behind her a car slowed.

Nothing unusual with that alone, but the fact there wasn't a car in front of it made her take note of it. Only when it didn't pass her like the others, nearly slowing to a crawl, did her instincts kick into high gear.

Ears tuned to the vehicle behind her, she slid her phone into her back pocket and scoped out a good hiding place should she need it. Just ahead was a gas station. Across the street, a wooded lot crowded with trees.

Her heart picked up speed, and she reached up to touch the comforting reassurance of her weapon tucked into the shoulder holster.

Two other cars passed by. The one trailing her slowed even more. She readied herself to spin and see if she could identify the person behind the wheel. For three more steps she kept her gaze forward.

Paige came to an abrupt stop, spun and squinted through the darkness. With a squeal of tires, the car jerked ahead before she could see the driver. Her pulse pounded, and she swiped her palms on her black sweats.

Her eyes on the fading taillights, she couldn't see the plate well enough, but thought she saw the letter *Z*. Not only that, but the car was white and looked suspiciously familiar. Could it be the same car that had tried to run Will down?

Watching it until the vehicle turned right a few streets up, she continued her brisk walk, senses alert, eyes probing the area around her. She'd be ready if the driver decided to make a loop and come back.

Finally, she arrived at the school without another incident. Taking a deep breath, she scoped the area. No one around that she could see. Paige skirted the edge of the fence and made her way to the side door.

Pulling out her key, she unlocked it, then went straight to the keypad and punched in the code. It blinked red once more, then turned green.

She was in. Locking the door behind her, she turned and faced the hallway.

Now for the search.

She wanted to start at one end of the building and go methodically through each classroom, looking for evidence of drugs and anyone involved in dealing them.

Light filtered through the halls, not as bright as they were during the day, but she could see well enough to make her way without pulling out the flashlight yet. She'd probably need that in the classrooms.

Paige pulled out the key the superintendent had given her—the master key—and inserted it in the door of the first classroom at the end of the hall.

Slipping inside, she grabbed the flashlight from her belt and clicked it on. She headed for the desk, her steps light and quick. Paige had no intention of sticking around any longer than necessary. She opened drawers, file cabinets and every place she thought might be a good hiding place for drugs.

Nothing.

And so it went for the next seven classrooms.

Forty-five minutes later, she stepped into the next room. Just as she shut the door behind her, she thought she heard a footstep in the hallway.

Dylan thought about the evening and everything he'd learned.

Paige was DEA.

Undercover at his nephew's school because she was after a killer and whoever was running drugs through the school.

Someone had broken into her house, had stolen the battery from her car and come back to her house for who knows what purpose and ended up breaking a window.

His mind reeled even as his gaze scanned the files he'd brought home.

He looked at the yellow legal pad to his right. Four names. Names of patients who might have a grudge against him for some reason.

His eyes blurred as exhaustion hit him. A glance at the clock showed it wasn't that late, but the past few restless, sometimes sleepless, nights had caught up with him.

Shoving the files to the side, he stood and walked out of the kitchen and down the hall to Will's room. The nightlight made the little boy's room glow, revealing the sleeping child.

Deciding to call it a night, Dylan readied himself for bed. He grabbed his Bible and settled himself in the recliner next to the window. This room was one of the reasons he'd purchased the house. The large master bedroom had enough room for his king-size bed, a recliner in front of the flat-screen television and a gas-log fireplace he used frequently during the winter months.

The only thing missing was someone to share it with.

At that thought, Paige's face came to the fore-front of his mind and he smiled. Then frowned. What he'd learned about her tonight was a lot to deal with. He closed his eyes. "Lord, guide me in the direction I'm supposed to go. You've placed Paige in my life for a reason. Show me what that is."

A noise sounded outside his bedroom, and he glanced at the door, expecting to see Will standing there, his silent expression asking Dylan to sit with him. Or the tear tracks on his cheeks indicative of yet another nightmare.

His eyes landed on empty space.

Setting the Bible on the small table next to the chair, Dylan stood and strode to the door. The deserted hallway greeted him. Pursing his lips, he walked down to Will's room.

Will's bed was vacant. That was odd.

"Will?"

A chill swept over him. Generally, Will didn't get out of bed unless it was to find Dylan or go to the bathroom. Dylan could see into the lighted restroom that Will used. He wasn't in there. Dylan frowned and considered what this might mean, even as he turned to search the rest of the house.

A quick scan of each bedroom made his heart thump faster. "Will? Where are you, buddy?"

He heard it again. A scrape.

Coming from the kitchen.

Spinning on his left foot, he charged toward the kitchen. Rounding the corner at the end of the hall, he cut through the den.

Another sound. He slowed, his senses taking in the noise. Will crying. That whimpering, lost sound that never failed to wrench Dylan's heart in two.

"Will?" he whispered.

Dylan approached the kitchen doorway, stopped and peered around the edge.

And froze.

Will stood with his back to Dylan, staring at the kitchen door—a large butcher knife clutched between both hands.

Paige stopped just inside the door, her fingers clutched around the knob. Her mind filtered through the list of people that might have a good reason for being at the school at ten o'clock on a Friday night.

She couldn't come up with one.

So, who had she heard outside in the hall?

Or had she actually heard a footstep?

Paige moved to the long vertical window by the door. The bottom half was covered with student work. The top half had a small area where she could look out.

Clipping her flashlight back onto her belt, she reached up with her left hand and unclipped the strap that held her weapon in the holster.

Grabbing her gun could possibly be considered

paranoid behavior, but after the events of the past few days, she would rather be paranoid than dead.

Peering through the window, she saw nothing in the dimly lit hallway.

But her instincts still shouted at her.

Someone was out in the hallway, and the memory of the car following behind her as she walked still crowded her mind.

Turning the knob, she opened the door with a click that sounded like an explosion in the silence. She flinched and froze.

Her ears strained to listen, and she thought she heard a shuffle. A muffled footstep?

Only one way to find out.

Opening the door wide enough to slip out, she paused one more time, heart humming, blood pumping in her veins. As soon as she shut the door, it would click again. An idea occurred to her. Slipping off her left shoe, she removed her sock and dropped it to the ground. All the while, she never took her eyes off the hallway. She replaced her shoe then waited.

After about a minute, she eased the door shut behind her. It was stopped by the sock and stayed silent.

In the hallway, she looked to her left—the direction she needed to go to get out of the building. Then to her right. And saw a shadow flash at the end of the hall.

Paige started toward it. Her hand gripped her weapon. Who would be here at this time of the night, sneaking around?

Besides her?

Slowly, she stalked the shadow, drawing closer, waiting for it to move again, desperately hoping it's owner didn't have a weapon. Out in the open hallway, she felt exposed, vulnerable. If whoever lurked ahead decided to take a shot at her, she was toast.

Her phone vibrated, and she froze trying to remember if she had it set to ring after two vibrations or not. Unwilling to take the chance it would ring, she shot one more glance toward the place where she'd seen the shadow, then grabbed her phone from her back pocket.

Pressing a button, she silenced the device without looking down.

Taking light steps toward where she'd last seen the shadow, she forced herself to breathe slow, pulling in deep, measured breaths. Her ears strained, her eyes probed. Her heart thudded in her chest.

And her phone vibrated.

A clatter ahead of her made her jump. Goose bumps popped out over her body.

Then the shadow was in front of her, darting toward her.

Paige flung herself around the corner into the

next hall and waited, chest heaving with adrenaline. She pulled her gun from her holster and held it steady.

"Who's there?" she called.

No answer. She hadn't really expected one.

Something held her back from identifying herself. If the shadow was someone on staff at the school, Paige didn't want to blow her cover.

And yet, she might have to.

Running footsteps snagged her attention and she peered around the corner to see the figure disappear down another hall.

Paige gave chase.

Heard a door open, then clank shut. An outside door.

The shadow was gone, no longer in the building. She reached the door and shoved it open, being careful to keep to the side, out of the line of fire.

Looking left, nothing. Right, the same. Whoever had been in the building had most likely disappeared into the trees bordering the school's property.

Did she continue to hunt him down?

Pulling back, she stared at the ceiling. No, he was gone. Finding someone dressed in black in the woods in the dark of night? Impossible without help—like dogs and lights and backup.

Her adrenaline rush began to ebb, and she

pulled her phone from her pocket to see who needed her so urgently.

Dylan.

The text read, Will needs you. Come ASAP.

# NINE

Dylan stood in the corner of the kitchen as Will gripped the knife, the little knuckles white and strained. "Will, I need you to put the knife on the counter, okay?"

How long could the little guy continue to stand there holding the heavy kitchen utensil? Dylan's heart banged a fast rhythm in his chest. What was he supposed to do? How could he help Will? What was going on in the boy's mind?

From a clinical standpoint, Dylan could see Will's pulse throbbing in his neck. His chest heaved with some emotion Dylan couldn't identify, although he thought it might be fear.

And anger.

Beneath it all, he could see the anger in the little boy.

And Dylan didn't blame him. "Will, it's okay, just put the knife down, please."

Dylan glanced at the phone he'd laid on the counter. He'd already texted Paige three times.

What was she doing? She was DEA, but she was also trained to work with traumatized children. And Will seemed to trust her.

Dylan wanted her here. Now. "Hey, buddy, you want me to try Paige again?"

The knife lowered.

Dylan took that as an affirmative and nearly shouted with relief. Finally, a breakthrough.

He reached for his phone and it buzzed in his hand. Out loud, he read, "I'm on my way."

Will's eyes went to the window, the door and then landed back on Dylan.

"Will, are you afraid?" Surely Will didn't think Dylan was going to hurt him? Dylan's heart nearly exploded with pain at the thought.

The little boy's eyelids flickered. His breath puffed in and out. Turning his back on Dylan, he walked to the kitchen table, grabbed a chair and pulled it toward the back door. Dylan stepped toward him. "Want some help?"

What was the child doing? And where was Paige?

Will ignored him but kept the knife in his right hand, the chair clutched in his left.

Dylan considered going up behind Will and grabbing the knife from him, and yet Will obviously wasn't ready to give it up. And Dylan didn't want to scare him by sneaking up on him. As long as it looked like he wasn't going to hurt himself, he'd let him hang on to it.

Finally, Will had the chair where he wanted it. He climbed up to look out the window.

Dylan stepped toward him until he was just a few feet away. "Did you see someone out there?"

Still, the child stared out the window, not acknowledging Dylan's presence.

A knock on the front door made them both jump, and Will let out a sound that was a cross between a grunt and a groan as he turned to stare in the direction of the foyer.

Dylan backed up, not taking his eyes from his nephew. "It's just Paige. I'm going to let her in. Okay?"

Will blinked and some of the terror fled his features.

Dylan made his way to the front door, still keeping Will in his line of vision. He made a quick check that it was Paige then flung the door open.

"What's wrong?" she asked as she stepped inside.

"In the kitchen. Will's having some sort of..." What should he call it? A breakdown? A panic attack? "...something."

He strode the three steps back into the kitchen with Paige on his heels. Her light scent drifted toward him, and he breathed in the comfort of it, thankful she was here.

\* \* \*

Paige stepped around him and drew in a breath at the sight of Will on the chair, big knife clutched in his little hand. Her mind clicked with her training. How to approach him? She knew something of his personality, knew he'd suffered a trauma, knew he needed understanding. "Hello, Will." She kept her voice soft, non-jarring, non-threatening.

His stance shifted, some of the tension easing from him. "Hey, little man, your uncle Dylan seems to think you want me here. What can I do for you?"

He licked his lips, and his eyes flicked toward the door, then back to her.

Paige could still see the lingering terror in his eyes. Something had scared him. Terrified him. "Can you give me the knife and trust me to keep you safe?"

Paige waited for what seemed like an eternity as she watched him think about it. Finally, he nodded and held the knife out toward her.

Dylan's harsh sigh made her blink, but she refused to look behind her, keeping her eyes trained on Will. She stepped forward and took the knife from his fingers.

His little face crumpled, and he began to cry, deep, silent sobs that nearly tore her heart from her chest.

Turning, Paige handed the knife to Dylan who took it and used his shirtsleeve to wipe the sweat from his forehead. Her heart clenched at the lost look in his eyes.

Anger, swift and hot, flowed through her at the person doing this to this little family.

Then Will claimed her attention as his little arms wrapped around her waist, and he rested his head against her belly. Holding him against her, she raised her eyes to meet Dylan's. Tears stood in his, and he shook his head in a helpless gesture.

Paige let Will cry for a good minute, then cupped his wet cheeks in her palms and lifted his face. Using her thumbs, she swiped the tears and told him, "It's going to be okay." Part of her felt a bit of guilt for telling him that, but she had a feeling that's what he needed to hear right now.

She felt a touch on her arm and looked up to see Dylan motioning her toward the den. Taking Will's hand in hers, she led him to the sofa and settled on it. Will climbed up beside her and rested his head against her. She wrapped an arm around him and within minutes, he was snoring gently.

Dylan sank onto the sofa, sandwiching Will between them. He stared at her over the little boy's head and whispered, "I'm sorry for my frantic texts. I wasn't sure what to do. He had that knife and..." He broke off and closed his eyes. "I knew

I could get it from him if I needed to, but I think he *needed* me to let him keep it."

Paige's heart went out to the man struggling so hard to do what was right for his nephew. "I'm so sorry. And I don't mind helping whenever I can." She leaned Will against his uncle. "Here, let him lean against you. I want to look around outside."

Dylan started. "You really think there was someone out there?"

"I don't know. I guess it wouldn't hurt to find out because something sure scared him." As she shifted the little boy onto his uncle's chest, his fingers grazed her cheek.

The spark that arced between them took her breath away, and she gulped. Her lungs struggled to remember how to function, and her pulse skipped a happy beat. The smokey look in his eyes said he felt the exact same thing she did.

Paige cleared her throat and looked at Will, trying to force a coherent thought into a brain that seemed to have short-circuited.

Dylan let her off the hook by changing the subject back to more serious matters. A fact for which she was grateful. He said, "Will was worried about the back door. If he saw something, it was out there."

She frowned. "In the garage?"

"Yeah. I hadn't shut the garage door yet so anyone could have walked inside." Paige grimaced and watched Dylan flush. Before she could say anything, he held up a hand. "I know. I should have closed it the minute we pulled in. I'm just not used to…looking over my shoulder."

Paige stood. "I hate to say it, but until we figure out what's going on around this little town, you might want to start." She looked at Will, then back at Dylan. "Do you know how long he was in the kitchen?"

"Not entirely. I thought he was asleep in his bed. I only came in here because I heard a noise. It was him."

She nodded. "All right. I'll be right back."

Slipping out the door, she removed the strap over her weapon and skirted around to the garage.

Looking for anything out of the ordinary, Paige scanned the area around the house.

Spying nothing there, she worked her way into the garage. The light came on, and she saw Dylan framed in the window. He opened the door and stood there, watching her. Examining the garage.

She spotted her mangled bike leaning against the wall and grimaced. "You would have been justified in sending it to the dump."

He shrugged. "It looks pretty expensive. If you can have it repaired…"

Lifting a brow, she shook her head. "I don't think that's going to be possible."

Then he said, "Over there, beside the gas can."

"What?"

"It's dirt."

She glanced at him. "And that's unusual in your garage?"

A smile curved his lips, but it had no humor in it. "It is when I just cleaned the garage early this morning before I took Will to school. There's no reason for it to be in here."

"What about Will's shoes? What if he was playing at school and—"

Dylan was shaking his head. "No. I'm telling you, that wasn't there when I walked in the house a few hours ago."

"Okay, then my guess is Will saw someone in the window of that door, and it terrified him. He grabbed the knife…"

"But why wouldn't he give it to me? Why wouldn't he hand it over when I asked him for it?"

Paige frowned, thinking. "Did he act threatening toward you?"

"No, not at all. It was like he was torn. He wanted to check the door, but he didn't want to leave me…." Again, he trailed off.

"Do you think he felt like *he* needed to protect *you* for some reason?"

Dylan blew out a sigh. "I can't imagine why. It makes no sense."

"I'm not saying that's what he was doing. It's just a theory."

Paige reentered the house and saw he'd covered Will with a blanket from the couch. Dylan looked at her. "He connects with you. Somehow, someway—in a way that I can't—he's picked you to bond with." Paige couldn't tell exactly how he felt about that, but it didn't seem to upset him or make him jealous.

He studied her for a few moments, then moved closer. She froze when he lifted a hand and placed it on her cheek. He whispered, "I don't blame him."

Paige felt her heart clog her throat as she met his eyes. "What do you mean?"

"I mean—" A flush crept into his cheeks and he looked like he wanted to bite his tongue. Instead, he cleared his throat and said, "I mean, I can't believe how God dropped you into my life right when I needed Him to."

"God?"

"Yes."

She smiled. "You know, I've been so busy building a life, climbing the career ladder, putting the bad guys in jail, I haven't really stopped to think about God much lately."

Dylan dropped his hand and led her over to the second couch facing the fireplace. She sat down and he scooted next to her. Very close to her. She almost asked him to move so she could think straight, then decided she liked having him so near.

He was saying, "You mentioned that your childhood wasn't exactly ideal. Can you tell me a little about it?"

The question jarred her. She didn't want to think about her lousy past. But she wanted something with this man. Something she wasn't sure she could have. Something she was scared to consider. "I grew up in a crack house, basically."

He choked. "A what?"

"It's not a pretty story, Dylan. It wasn't country club and tee times for me."

Incredulous, he just stared, then asked, "So how did you get from there to…here?"

Paige leaned her head back to stare at the ceiling. "There was a couple in our neighborhood, Mama Ida and Papa Stu. They could have probably lived anywhere they wanted to, but they chose to stay in that neighborhood and do their best to save the children."

"Missionaries?"

"Technically. I guess. They didn't call themselves missionaries, but they definitely did mission work. I would go over to their house every chance I got. My mom didn't care. She was strung out most of the time and didn't notice whether I came home or not."

"What about a grandparent or a family member? There was no one else you could have lived with?"

"No. As far as I know, my mother was an only child. And my grandmother was as bad as my mother, so…" She shrugged, the old shame creeping into her as she related her story. And if he knew about Ben, there was no way he'd want her taking care of Will. "Anyway, Mama Ida showed me there was another life, another world out there. I wanted what she had. She's the one who led me to Christ." Paige blew out a sigh. "Funny, I haven't thought about them in a while and now… All the memories are just flowing."

He reached over and squeezed her fingers. "Thanks for sharing that with me."

She nodded and he leaned forward, lips millimeters from her. Paige drew back. She glanced at Will and felt grief pierce her. "And that's why I'll never be a mother."

# TEN

So, he hadn't misunderstood. He watched as she left, his hopes crushed, mangled. She didn't want children. And he had a bad feeling there wasn't any way he was going to change her mind.

A heavy sigh escaped him. *Lord, I'm not sure what You're doing, but I sure wish You'd let me in on the plan. If Paige won't ever be a mother, then we can't ever be together. It's as simple as that. And yet, I thought You might be working something out between us. If You're not, then would You take away the growing feelings I have for her? They're making me crazy.*

Dylan figured God would reveal the reason He'd thrown he and Paige together at some point. But what if they weren't meant to be together? What if God had brought her into his and Will's life simply because He knew that she was the only person Will would respond to? What if Dylan didn't figure into the plan?

Despair hit him. God didn't work that way, did He?

He just wasn't sure. One thing about faith was accepting that you couldn't see the big picture. However, the one thing he was sure of was that God had a plan and whatever it was, it was the best thing for Dylan and Will. The thought reassured him somewhat.

As gently as possible, Dylan picked Will up from the couch and transferred him to the big king bed. Will didn't need to be alone tonight. Normally, Dylan firmly believed children belonged in their own beds, but tonight… Well, tonight was different. If Will woke from his nightmares, Dylan wanted to be right by his side.

Dylan settled himself into the recliner once again and grabbed his Bible from the nightstand. Between Will and Paige, Dylan's heart was on the world's record of roller-coaster rides.

Again, his mind circled to the fact that Paige felt she'd make a lousy mother. He couldn't grasp it. So she'd had a rotten childhood. A lot of people did. And they became parents. Some of them turned out to be good ones; some didn't. Dylan flashed to her tender care of Will, her concern about the children at the school and the possibility that someone was dealing drugs in a place that was supposed to be safe and nurturing.

She couldn't see it, but she would be a great mother.

*Lord, help me show her. But protect my heart if it's not to be.*

His brain worked on the problem.

And, slowly, a plan formed.

If God allowed it, Dylan wanted Paige in his life long enough to figure out if they could have a relationship worth fighting for. His gaze went to Will, still sleeping. He looked peaceful for once.

But how long would that last?

What had Will seen in the garage that had frightened him so much?

A chill settled around Dylan. Was it the same person that had set fire to his sister's house?

And if so, had Will seen the person responsible?

Dylan shuddered and determined to check into an alarm system first thing in the morning.

As a child, she used to hate Saturday mornings. It meant being home all day. No school meant no food most days. Summers had been the hardest. Thankfully, the sweet couple in her neighborhood had fed her at least one good meal each day when school was out.

For the first time in a long while, she thought

about her mother. Should she call her? Ask her if she needed anything?

Her gaze went to the phone and before she thought twice about it, she dialed the number.

"Hello?" The raspy voice from her childhood. It sent chills through her. "Who is this?"

She cleared her throat. "It's uh, me, Mom."

Silence. Then, "Well, well. Hello, Paige."

"How are you doing?"

"'Bout the same."

"You need anything?"

"Nope."

"Mom, I…"

"I'm good, Paige. I've come to realize something over the past few months. You don't owe me nothing."

A surprising statement from the woman who thought Paige owed her for the simple fact that she was alive and walking the earth. "That's not why I'm calling."

Why was she calling? Did she think her memories of her mother had been faulty in some way? That her mother had somehow developed the ability to love someone other than herself?

Maybe.

"Then what do you need, girl?"

"Just…just, will you call me if I can do anything?"

A hacking cough filtered through the line and

made Paige wince. Then her mother laughed. "You can send me some money. That's about all I need. At least for the next few months. Then I suppose you won't have to worry about me anymore."

"Mom…"

"See ya, Paige."

Click. Paige pulled the phone from her ear and stared at the screen.

Why did she even bother?

Yet a tiny part of her admitted she wanted her mother to tell her she loved her. Another part of her was mad that she cared.

Enough of the past. Paige shoved the thoughts away and focused on the present.

Standing off to the side, near the window, Paige sipped her coffee and looked out into the still dark street.

In a few minutes, she would call Charles and find out if he'd gotten a hit on the partial plate she'd given him. In addition to the plate, she'd added a vague description of the car. With those two things, he should be able to dramatically narrow down the list.

Then she would call Dylan and see if she could help him work on his files to come up with someone who had a grudge against him.

Still, something niggled at the back of her mind. She couldn't shake the feeling she was missing something. Something that should be obvious.

What was it?

Her phone rang and she jumped. Rolling her eyes at her reaction, she snatched the device from the counter.

Charles. He'd beat her to the draw.

She punched the button and said, "You're up early."

"I've got a case I want closed."

His gruff voice made her smile. Then she frowned. "What do you have?"

"Your plate and description of the car came up with only one possibility. Simon Moore."

She set her coffee down with a thud. It sloshed over the rim and burned her thumb. Ignoring it, she said, "The reporter."

"Yeah. I would tell you to let the sheriff haul him in so you could question him, but I'm not ready for you to break cover yet. So—" he blew out a breath "—I'm going to have one of our agents call him for questioning, and you can drive in to the Bryson City police department and do your thing. A detective will wear an earpiece and relay your questions to Mr. Moore."

"That sounds good." She could do that. "What about the footprint outside my window? Anything back from the lab on that?"

"They've got the cast of it. Size ten tennis shoe."

"So now I need to provide you a suspect so you can compare his shoes."

"Exactly."

"I'll get right on that."

She hung up. So, she wouldn't be going through files with Dylan today. The stinging disappointment surprised her. Then she chastised herself. Dylan had been transparent last night when he'd commented for the second time on the fact that she'd be a great mom.

It drove home the point.

She and Dylan weren't meant to be together.

And that hurt.

A lot.

When she was with him, she didn't want to leave. When she was away from him, he was constantly in the back of her thoughts. Or she was just plain thinking about him.

*God? I know I haven't been very communicative lately.* She paused. *And I'm sorry about that. Dylan's very committed to You. And I find that I really like that about him. It makes me want to know him more, but the whole mother thing... Well, you know how I feel about that. I've already failed once and...I'm just...afraid. There, I said it. So, now what?*

She waited, but didn't get an answer. Had she been expecting one? Maybe. She thought about the Stuarts. The family who'd taken her in and taught her about God. Told her she could be somebody different. Encouraged her to do well in school and get out of that neighborhood.

Mama Ida and Papa Stu. She'd been with them when Ben had stopped coughing. She hated to remember how she'd forgotten about him and enjoyed the company of Mama Ida and Papa Stu, while illness overtook his little body.

They'd be disappointed that she'd let her faith wane and her closeness with God dissipate. A lump formed in her throat, and she swallowed hard. Well, at least that was one thing she did have the power to change.

Shaking her head, pushing her personal thoughts aside for the moment, she dialed Dylan's number.

At the sound of his voice, her feelings for this man came flooding back. She pushed them away. She'd never allow herself to put a child's well-being in her hands. Not after she'd followed her mother's example and ignored the suffering of another child in the next room. The police hadn't found her mother at fault, but Paige knew differently. Both she and her mother had been guilty of neglect. But she was only eight years old. The reasonable part of her mind knew that she couldn't be held responsible. But her heart had a hard time accepting it.

* * *

When she'd explained to Dylan her plans for the morning had changed, he'd insisted on changing his, too. He'd arranged for a babysitter for Will and met her in front of her house.

"Hop in, I'll drive."

Hesitating, she bit her lip. "I don't know, Dylan, I'm not sure this is a good idea."

His eyes hardened. "If he was the man at my house the other night, I need to know. Someone is terrorizing my nephew, and I refuse to sit by twiddling my thumbs when I can be proactive."

Paige saw the determination on his face and figured she might as well just give in gracefully. If he wanted to go, why not?

"We don't know that this is the person who was at your house."

"But he could be."

He waited. Blowing out a sigh of surrender, she climbed in. At least she would have company on the way.

Good company.

Company she didn't think she'd ever grow tired of.

As he drove, Paige kept an eye on the rearview and side mirrors. Just because they had someone in custody didn't mean they had the *right* someone.

"Do you ever wonder what your mother's doing now?"

The question jolted her. "What?"

"Your mother. You're not even curious how she's doing?"

Paige pursed her lips. "When you've been hurt by someone as much as she's hurt me, at some point you just kind of…write that person off."

No point in mentioning the phone call this morning. She was still processing the hurt, trying to push it behind the wall that had her mother's name on it.

"I'm sorry," he said.

She shrugged. "It is what it is. I don't let it bother me that much." *Liar.*

"So you know where she is?"

"I do."

"Oh."

He drove in silence for about ten minutes. Paige waited, and he didn't disappoint her. "Where is she?"

"In the same nasty little house I grew up in." Paige paused. "She has terminal liver cancer and about two more months to live according to the last report I got from the doctor who agreed to talk to me. For what it's worth, I offered to let her come live with me, and she turned me down. End of story."

"I—"

"Please. Let's just change the subject, okay?"

Her mother's rejection still stung. It shouldn't, but it did.

"Sure."

"Did you get an alarm system put in?" she asked.

"They're working on it even as we speak."

"Good."

They rode in silence for the rest of the ride.

Paige could feel Dylan's tension and felt her own stress rise as a result.

Located on Main Street, the two-story, Bryson City Police Department building looked new.

Wheeling into the parking lot, Dylan found a spot near the door, and they climbed out. Once inside the building, she gave her name, flashed her badge and, within minutes, she and Dylan were greeted by Chief Zachary Bennett.

"He came down voluntarily when we told him we had a few questions for him," the chief said.

Paige chewed her bottom lip as she considered how to go about this. "I want to do this without blowing my cover, if at all possible. My boss said he'd arranged for me to wear an earpiece and feed questions about what to ask Mr. Moore."

"He did." The chief motioned for one of his officers and put in the request. The officer left to do his bidding, and Chief Bennett showed Paige and Dylan into an observation room.

Paige made herself comfortable in one of the padded chairs. Dylan followed her lead and lowered himself into the one next to hers. Through the two-way mirror, she could see Simon Moore seated at the lone table in the interrogation room. His right leg jiggled under the table, and he chewed a nail on his left hand.

The chief spoke. "Detective Means is getting fitted with the earpiece now. He'll be questioning Mr. Moore."

"Did you get a search warrant for his place?"

"Sure did. I've got officers there now. If they find anything worth noting, one of them will either call or bring it by. He lives about ten minutes from here."

"We're specifically looking for a shoe to match up with a cast we got outside a window."

"Yeah, that's what your boss said." The chief stood to the side. "We didn't have time to run a test, so ask him to show you he can hear you when he gets in there."

Paige nodded and sat back. She was ready.

A short wait later, the door opened and Detective Means walked in, looking relaxed. If she didn't know better, she'd think he was ready for a picnic in the park.

Paige tensed and spoke into the small microphone. "Rub your nose if you can hear me."

Detective Means scratched the edge of his nose as though it itched.

From the corner of her eye, she could see Dylan

watching her. His expression remained unreadable, thoughtful. She wanted to know what he was thinking. Did he regret coming with her?

She couldn't worry about that now.

But she did wonder.

Dylan was thinking he'd gotten himself involved with a woman who confused him on just about all levels. On the one hand, he'd seen her vulnerable and hurt. And in hindsight, he realized she'd just been doing her job when she pushed through her pain to question him about his sister and the fire when all she probably wanted to do was curl up and go to sleep.

On the other hand, he'd seen her determined to catch the man who'd tried to break into her house—and the steel in her eyes when she'd silently conveyed to him to keep his mouth shut with Eli.

And now this. He needed a third hand. Here she was the consummate professional, ready to question the man on the other side of the mirror via the technology provided—without breaking her cover.

Simply put, she was amazing. And everything he'd ever wanted in a woman.

Except for one insurmountable obstacle.

She didn't want to be a mother.

And he'd never give up Will.

Not even for her.

Not that she'd ever ask him to do that. Because in the short amount of time he'd known her, he'd realized something about her that she probably didn't even recognize about herself.

She was one of the most giving, selfless people he'd ever met.

The chief left the small room, then Paige's voice made him blink. She was saying, "Ask him why his blood was found on the glass he broke trying to get into my house."

A little *gotcha* smile played on her lips. She looked like the proverbial cat who'd caught the doomed canary.

Simon froze. "What?" His left hand went to his right elbow. He stared into the detective's eyes a moment longer, then his shoulders slumped.

"Got him," Paige whispered.

"Why?" Dylan asked.

She glanced at him. "We've got his DNA. He knows it and we know it. Now, it's just a matter of if he's willing to talk without a lawyer present."

Simon stood and paced to the small window. His chin barely topped the sill. "All right. I was there."

Paige bolted to her feet. "Ha. I knew it."

"We know you were there." Detective Means leaned forward, placing his palms on the table as he watched Simon pace back to the chair. "We also have a partial plate that matches your vehicle."

The reporter waved a hand. "Okay, I get it. You've got me cold."

"You'd better believe it."

Paige shot him a grin, and Dylan couldn't help the answering smile. The high she got catching bad guys must be the same one he got helping people heal.

Into the microphone, she said, "Ask him what he was doing there. What does Paige Worth have that he wants?"

The detective asked.

The reporter snorted. "A story. What else?" He spread his hands. "I'm simply after a story."

"Then why try to break in Dylan Seabrook's home last night?" Paige fed him the question.

Simon jerked. "What? I didn't."

Derision filled Detective Means's face. "Come on, Moore, you can do better than that."

"Seriously, I wasn't even in Rose Mountain last night, and I can prove it."

"But you admit the attempted break-in at Ms. Worth's house."

Moore sighed and closed his eyes. "Yes. I mean no. I mean—"

"Come on. It has to be one or the other."

"Yes, I was there that night. No, I wasn't trying to break in."

The chief popped his head in the door, and Dylan watched him give a thumbs up to Paige. "We've got a shoe that matches the cast."

Satisfaction curled through Dylan. So, all of the crazy incidents that had happened over the past few days were caused by that man. A reporter.

"But why?"

Paige overheard his whispered question and nodded indicating the detective was getting to that.

When asked the question, Simon Moore grimaced, then gave a sheepish grin. "For a story, of course." He shrugged. "Ms. Worth wouldn't talk to the reporters after she saved the kid's life. I figured if I got the scoop, well…"

"It wouldn't hurt your career any."

The reporter flushed. "Yeah. At her house, I was just trying to get a picture, overhear some conversation, whatever. Then I slipped, and my elbow went through the window."

"What about Dylan's office last week? What were you looking for?" Paige asked into the microphone.

The detective blinked, but didn't change expression. He transferred the question to Simon.

Simon's flush deepened, confirming Paige's suspicions. "I was looking for his schedule, his home address. Anything that would lead me to where he had the kid."

"But you weren't at his house last night?" Detective Means didn't bother to hide his skepticism.

"No," the reporter insisted. "I wasn't there." He set his jaw. "And I'm not saying I was just because you want it to be true."

Dylan believed the man. He didn't want to, but he did.

But if it hadn't been Simon Moore in his garage last night, who had scared Will?

# ELEVEN

Dylan absently stroked his cheek as he drove.

Paige eyed the sky. "More rain."

"You sound disgusted."

"A little. The weather's been pretty bad off and on for the past few weeks."

He saw her gaze flick to the rearview mirror. She was still alert, still worried about something if the lines on her forehead were any indication.

He wasn't sure why.

The interrogation had determined that Simon Moore had not only been the man outside Paige's house that night, but he'd also tried to sneak into her room at the hospital. He'd looked familiar to Dylan, and when he'd asked Paige to pass that question on to the detective, Moore confirmed it.

He supposed she was still anxious because they still didn't know who had been driving the car in the school zone that nearly killed Will and Paige. Moore's white car showed no signs of damage, nor had it been fixed since the hit-and-run. Which meant they also still didn't know who had been outside in his garage last night.

He sighed and looked at the woman beside him. "Cheryl, my housekeeper—and friend—has Will. She has to take her husband to the doctor, so she's going to drop off Will to me."

"Why don't you ask her to bring him to wherever his favorite fast-food restaurant is? He can play while we work."

He thought about that. So, she wasn't in any hurry to part company with him. Was it because she wanted to be with him, or because she really thought they could figure something out?

"I can have Cheryl bring the file that I found that has the most potential for someone to have a grudge against me."

She flashed him a smile. "That'd be great."

Dylan got on the phone and made the arrangements.

Even while he was on the phone with Cheryl, his heart picked up speed at the thought of spending the rest of the day with Paige.

Then Will's face flashed across his mind and his stomach plunged. *Please Lord, show me what You want. Don't let me fall for another woman who won't fit into our lives.*

Throwing up the walls around his heart, he pulled into the parking lot and found a spot near the door.

Cheryl had beat him here. Her car was three spaces down.

Once inside the restaurant, Will spotted Paige first and darted to her side. He stood there staring at her. She smiled and reached out to give the little boy a hug. Will squeezed her neck, then turned to look at Dylan. Dylan nodded to the playground area and Will took off.

Paige greeted Cheryl with a smile and a short hug. "Thanks again for arranging to fill my freezer. I won't have to cook for a year."

Cheryl laughed. "It was our pleasure. We're happiest when feeding someone."

Knowing Cheryl needed to get going, Dylan said, "Thanks so much for keeping him this morning."

"It's never a problem. You know I consider that boy like one of my own grandchildren."

Dylan gave her a hug and asked Paige, "Will you keep an eye on Will while I walk her to her car?"

"Sure."

Dylan delivered Cheryl to her car, and she handed him the file. "She's pretty."

He raised what he hoped was innocent brow. "Yes, I'd noticed that."

"Whew. That's a relief. I was afraid you were going to pine away for Erica forever."

"Pine away? I hardly think so."

Cheryl simply grunted, gave him a half grin, climbed into her car and drove off.

The back of Dylan's neck tingled, and he looked around, wondering why he would feel as though someone was watching him. His gaze took in the action going on, and nothing looked out of place. No one seemed to be staring at him. Yet goose bumps popped out on his arms, and a sense of foreboding covered him.

Hurrying back into the restaurant, Dylan set the file on the table and slid in the booth opposite her even while his eyes probed the play area, easily spotting Will on the kid-size, rock-climbing wall. His heart calmed, and he shrugged off his unease. To Paige, he said, "You picked a good spot. We'll be able to talk, and I'll be able to see Will at the same time."

A smile curved her lips. "No problem." Her eyes landed on the file. "What do you have?"

"A possibility."

She arched a brow at him. "Why don't you tell me about it?"

Dylan sighed and opened the file to the first page. "It was my first year in practice on my own. A man brought his wife in with severe, abdominal pain. After ruling out ectopic pregnancy, miscarriage and other possible causes for the pain, I told him I thought she had appendicitis, and that he needed to go into Bryson City for an ultrasound.

He refused, wanted me to treat her in my office."
Dylan closed his eyes and shook his head. "As I
was explaining why I couldn't perform surgery,
her appendix ruptured. And still the man argued
with me."

"What happened?"

"She died."

Paige winced. "Oh, no, that's awful."

"It's the only case I can think of where someone might have a grudge against me."

He watched her rummage in her purse and
come up with a pen and small notebook. "Give
me the name and contact information of the husband, and I'll pass it on to Charles. He can have
someone investigate what this guy's been up to
the past few days."

Dylan gave the information. She tucked it away
and pushed a strand of hair behind her ear. Every
once in a while, her gaze would flick over to Will,
watching him play, and a soft light would momentarily light her eyes before she looked back at him.

"You know, Will's been seeing a therapist ever
since the fire."

She started. "No, I didn't know that." A pause.
"I mean, I think you mentioned something about
some counseling, but you never gave me the details."

"She's someone who was recommended to me

by my pastor. He suggested someone with play-therapy experience."

"That's a good idea. Play therapy can be a great, nonthreatening way to get kids to open up. I use it myself when I have to interrogate a child."

"He's not responding to her."

"Oh. Did you tell her about the situation with the knife?"

His eyes searched hers. "No. I'm not taking him back to her. I want you to work with him."

She simply stared at him and he shifted, uncomfortable with her direct gaze.

"But I'm really not qualified—"

"Look." He held out a beseeching hand. "Will has taken to you from the moment he saw you. I don't know why, I don't know what's going on in his mind. But I see it, and I want to take advantage of that. Will you try to find out what he saw the night of the fire?"

Paige sucked in a deep breath. She knew he was right. Will *was* drawn to her for some reason. Maybe it was the fact that she'd saved his life. She didn't know. One thing she *was* sure of was that she needed to keep digging. Not only with Will, but with the staff at the school. She needed to take this opportunity to learn more about what Will knew, but what if she couldn't help him?

"Dylan, I…"

Commotion from the playground area snapped her head up. A man in a dark shirt and a baseball cap had a child in his arms.

And was heading for the Emergency Exit. The alarm sounded.

Other children pointed and yelled.

The child struggled, the terror on his familiar face saying he didn't want to go with the man who held him.

"Will!"

Dylan was already racing for the play area.

Paige snatched Dylan's keys from the table and bolted for the door, her plan to go around the side and trap the man in the middle. Or follow him in the car if she wasn't fast enough.

Already he was out the door, the crowd watching in horror as the kidnapping unfolded. One young mother tried to stop the large man and earned a punch to the face for her efforts. She dropped like a rock to the floor.

Through the glass, Paige could see Dylan having trouble wading through those crowded around trying to see the action. Her gaze fixed on the man hurrying Will to his car. He tossed the boy in the car and yelled something at him.

She saw Will roll over the front seat into the back and disappear from view. Rage and sheer terror filled her. If the man managed to drive off—

Paige figured she had only one option.

Bolting to Dylan's car, she slid in and rammed the key in the ignition and shoved the car into reverse. Pressing the gas pedal, she squealed from the parking spot, threw the car in Drive and headed straight for the car that now held Will and his kidnapper.

# TWELVE

Dylan finally managed to push his way through the gawking crowd, only to find he was too late. Fear like he'd never felt before screamed through him. "Will!"

Screeching tires and the sound of colliding bumpers rent the air, and Dylan watched as Paige jumped from his car to race toward the one that she'd just stopped head-on.

A figure bolted from the other car and took off toward the row of stores lining the parking lot. Dylan let him go without a second thought; his sole focus was getting to Will. The crash seemed minor, but it had been a major risk to cause an accident with Will in the car.

Paige caught his eye and motioned she was going after the man. Torn, he wanted to tell her to stay put, to not place herself in danger. However, he knew she wouldn't listen. And Will was his main concern at the moment. He nodded, shot her a please-be-careful look that she didn't catch as she'd already taken off in pursuit of the man.

Arriving at the car, he found Will hunched in the backseat, his shoulders shaking, tears streaming down his pale cheeks. "Will. Hey, it's okay." Dylan placed a hand on the boy's back, and Will jerked, his head shooting up. Seeing Dylan, he launched himself into his arms.

Dylan pulled him from the car and turned to find three police cars in the parking lot, lights flashing.

"Which way did he go?" one deputy asked.

Dylan pointed in the direction he'd seen Paige bolt.

His arms clutched his nephew; rage boiled beneath the surface. If he got his hands on the person responsible for terrorizing his nephew, he'd probably kill him.

Paige dodged a pedestrian as she desperately tried to keep the fleeing kidnapper in sight. Concern over Will's safety was pushed to the back burner as determination to catch the man fueled her faster. Without pause, he pushed past two ladies exiting a store, never stopping as they expressed their outrage.

Paige followed with a muttered, "Excuse me."

And came to an abrupt halt.

Her eyes scanned the store. A woman pulling

a dress off the rack. A toddler ducking under his mother's legs.

But no man in a black T-shirt and a baseball cap.

Where had he gone?

She whirled in full circle, eyes probing each face. Striding toward the back entrance, she pulled her cell phone from her pocket and dialed 911. As soon as the operator came on the line, she blurted, "I saw a kidnapper. He raced into Maguire's Clothing on Twenty-ninth. I think he might go out the back and try to get away." She could see the flashing lights in the parking lot of the restaurant.

Paige hung up. She needed to make a decision. Head for the back door and see if the man had gone out, or go back out the front and try to cut him off. But if he'd gone out the back, she would be too late.

But what if he was hiding behind a rack of clothes? If she wanted to blow her cover, she'd immediately call for the store to be shut down.

But it might be too late anyway.

And she wasn't ready to give up her cover yet.

Slowly, she made her way to the back of the store, noting the security cameras.

"May I help you?"

Paige turned to see the questioning expression on the clerk's young face. She couldn't be more than twenty-one. Paige nodded. "Did you see a guy come through here with a baseball cap on?"

A frown drew her perfectly arched brows together over her nose. "No, I'm sorry. I didn't see anyone."

Frustration bit at her. So, did he go out the back or not? "Does your back door have an alarm on it?"

"Only at night. Why?"

Paige realized she sounded too much like a cop. But she had to know. "Because a guy tried to kidnap a little boy a few minutes ago, and he ran in here."

The clerk gasped. "You're kidding!"

"So, the door wasn't alarmed?"

"No, during the day, we leave it off because we get deliveries and employees use that door."

Paige grimaced. He was long gone by now.

There was nothing left to do but head back to the restaurant and see how Dylan and Will were.

She thanked the woman and started to leave. If it were up to her, she'd question everyone in the store, but she couldn't. It wasn't her job. It was Eli's. An idea struck her.

She turned back to the clerk. "Um, you're going to think I'm crazy, but do you think you could get everyone's name and contact information in case the police want to talk to them? I mean he did run in this store, and someone might have noticed something."

"Are you a cop?"

"Just a concerned citizen who watches too much cop television." Paige gave a weak smile and left before she completely blew her cover.

When she arrived back at the restaurant, Dylan still clutched Will, and it looked like Will had no intention of letting go of his uncle anytime soon.

Eli stood on the sidewalk directing the investigation. Just as she walked up, she heard him tell Dylan, "A forensics team from Asheville is on the way. They're coming by helicopter so they'll be here shortly. I'll have one of my deputies meet them at the landing area."

Paige looked at the crunched bumpers. Everything in her wanted to go over there and search the vehicle.

Eli looked at her and frowned. "What do you think you're doing chasing after a kidnapper?"

Paige opened her mouth then closed it. Then opened it. "I didn't really think about it. I just did it."

His eyes narrowed. "That was some pretty quick thinking ramming his car. And I don't know if that was brave or stupid of you to go chasing after him." Suspicion glinted in the depths of his green eyes and she knew he had a plethora of questions running around in his cop brain.

She gave a weak shrug. "Thanks. I just couldn't let him drive off with Will. I figured he'd be better off bumped and bruised a little, rather than gone." She shuddered. "The kidnapper ran in that store but I couldn't catch him before he ran out the back."

"And my guys weren't here fast enough." Eli's tight jaw looked like it might shatter. He looked around and motioned for two officers. "Go question the people in the store. I want to know everything they know."

Paige felt a surge of satisfaction. Eli was a good cop.

Dylan grabbed her in a hug and whispered in her ear, "That's twice you've saved him."

Paige placed her hand on Will's head and gave thanks for his safety. *Thank You for putting me here, God.*

She jolted at the prayer that seemed to come from nowhere. And then smiled. She supposed Dylan was having more of an effect on her than she would have thought.

As she studied the car, a sense of foreboding curled through her. It was white. She wondered if the front bumper had a dent in it before she had rammed it.

Paige elbowed Dylan. "Does that look like the same car from the school?"

His eyes narrowed on it and she watched him swallow hard. "Yes, it sure does."

Dylan raked a hand through his hair. After two hours' worth of statements, questioning and hanging around to see if they could find out anything new about the man who had tried to snatch Will, Dylan was just plain exhausted.

But grateful that Eli had promised to get back with him on any new developments.

Medical school had been a breeze compared to the past few days.

And they still needed to eat.

Although Will hadn't said anything, he was cranky in his silent-Will way. Shifting, sagging, refusing to walk and clinging to Dylan were all pretty good indicators that the child had had his fill of adventure—and terror—today.

Dylan was ready to join him. "Hey, big guy, how about those chicken nuggets now? I bet you're starving."

Will froze, his eyes wide, yearning.

Dylan gave him a squeeze. "I'll take that as a yes." He looked at Paige who stood watching them. "Let me get us all some food, and we can pick up where we left off."

She nodded. "Sounds good." As he carried Will to the counter to order, he saw Paige pull her phone from her pocket, punch a few buttons, then hold the device to her ear.

Who was she calling?

"Sir? May I take your order?" Pulling his thoughts from whoever was on the other end of the line he placed his order.

By the time he returned to the table, Will had finally turned loose his death grip and was willing to slide into the booth.

Paige was no longer on the phone, she was studying the file he'd left on the table in his rush to rescue Will. Looking up, she glanced at the child, then at Dylan. "We could go eat somewhere else."

Dylan paused. "I know. I thought about it. But then he'll be afraid of ever coming in here again. And there's no reason to be afraid. The bad man's gone." His words answered her question but were directed at Will. "Right Will?"

Will seemed to think about that as he watched Dylan distribute the food. His eyes went to the playground area where three children played and giggled.

Apparently deciding his uncle made sense, some of the tension left his shoulders, and he dipped his first nugget into the barbecue sauce.

Dylan looked at Paige.

She grinned at him, and he felt his heart thud

a little faster. It was a good thing she turned her attention back to the file in front of her.

Paige read for a full five minutes, taking bites of her sandwich every so often. Looking up, she finally said, "I can see why you might think this person would have a grudge against you. This happened quite a while ago, though. It doesn't make sense that he would come after you now."

Dylan shrugged. "I thought of that. The only thing I could come up with was that he obsessed over her loss, decided I was to blame and is now out to take away—" he paused and cut a glance at Will, then finished "—the most important thing in my life."

Nodding, she shut the file. "While you were ordering the food, I called my boss and gave him a description of the car. And the license plate."

"Eli will take care of that, won't he?"

She smiled. "Yes, he will, and not to sound arrogant, but Charles has resources Eli doesn't. Before we leave, Charles'll probably call back with all kinds of information long before Eli has the plate run."

Even as the words left her mouth, the phone rang, and she gave a satisfied smile when she checked the screen. "Hi, Charles. You have some information for me?"

As she listened, Dylan looked at Will. The child had eaten all of his nuggets and had about three french fries left. Leaning over, Dylan asked, "If I check the playground for you and promise it's safe, you want to go play again?"

Will's eyes went wide. Dylan saw him gulp as his gaze flicked to the area where someone had tried to snatch him only hours before.

Paige finished her conversation, stood and held out her hand. "Come on. I'll show you that the bad man is all gone, and you can slide all you want."

Will still hesitated, his gaze swinging back and forth between the playground and Paige. She smiled at him. "Sometimes we have to face our fears to find out there's nothing there to be afraid of anymore."

Dylan jerked and looked at Will. Would he understand her soft words?

Something must have registered, because he rose from his seat and held out a hand to her. She grasped his fingers and led him to the play area. Warmth suffusing him, Dylan watched her take Will through the whole area, gently pointing out that he was safe.

Finally, she asked him something and Will nodded. Then threw himself at her, wrapping his small arms around her waist. Dylan's throat clutched at the scene. He knew Will missed his mother. Was the boy hoping Paige might take Sandra's place? The thought shot fear through him. Fear he might mess up, and Will would wind up scarred for life.

Swamped by self-doubt about letting Will care so much about a woman who declared that she'd never be a mother, Dylan wondered if he should cut off all contact between the two. At least until he was convinced Paige might stick around.

Seeing Will's smile as he climbed the plastic steps to slide down into Paige's waiting arms nearly did him in.

It was too late to do anything about keeping Will from Paige. She and the child had a special bond.

Now it was up to Dylan to convince Paige of that.

When she returned to the table, he couldn't take his eyes from her flushed cheeks. "Will is falling hard for you. You have a real connection with him."

For a moment she froze, her gaze on his food. "He's an easy child to love." Pulling in a deep breath, she cleared her throat, and Dylan had a feeling she was getting ready to change the subject. "So," she said, "tell me more about the people Sandra hung around with and any names she might have dropped while in your presence."

Sometimes Dylan hated being right.

# THIRTEEN

Monday morning, Paige blinked at the bright sunlight streaming through her office window. Disgust curled through her. So far, this case was coming up as one, big nothing. Charles had said the car the kidnapper drove was stolen. A forensics team from Asheville would go over it. When they had information for him, Paige would be the first to know.

On the plus side, yesterday she'd attended church with Dylan and Will and had been pleasantly surprised at the pastor's message.

He reminded her of the couple in her neighborhood who'd led her to Christ. Gentle, yet firm, never wavering, always consistent.

Something she'd desperately needed at that age.

Only now it was Monday, and Dylan had dug into his memory and come up with one name he thought might have had more than a professional relationship with his sister here at the school.

Jessica Stanton. The blonde teacher Paige had met in the lounge on her first day.

She really needed to dig deeper in Sandra's connections here at the school. She'd discovered Sandra subbed in all three schools in the small town and was well-known, but not exactly well thought of. She'd been subbing at Will's school the day of the fire.

A quick glance at the clock showed her it was one minute until ten o'clock. She'd already seen several children today and fortunately, none of them had serious issues. A fight with a sibling, a parent disappointed in a bad grade. Nothing she couldn't handle.

Now, she popped up from her desk and headed down the hall toward Jessica's classroom.

Paige arrived just in time to see the students lining up. Jessica spotted her and raised a brow. "Hi, can I do something for you?"

"Just thought I'd pop in and see if you'd like to grab a cup of coffee in the lounge."

A friendly smile sparked in the teacher's eyes, and she nodded to the kids. "Let me drop them off at the gym for PE, and I'll meet you there."

Three minutes later, Jessica entered the lounge, and Paige took a deep breath, getting into her role of concerned counselor. It wasn't hard. She was concerned. After they'd prepared their coffee, Jessica sat opposite Paige.

Fortunately, they were the only two in the lounge for now. If her observations were correct, it would get a little busy in the next few minutes.

"I've taken quite an interest in little Will Price. He's a cutie. I hear you were pretty close with his mother."

Pain flashed in Jessica's eyes. "Yes. She subbed here occasionally. Several times she was in the classroom next to mine, and we got to know each other. Even got together after school some days."

"I'd heard something like that. It's a horrible shame what happened to her."

"I know. I couldn't believe it. I was just… stunned. She was so happy, finally getting her life together and then…the fire." Jessica swallowed hard and shook her head.

Paige frowned. "I'm going to talk to Will in just a little while. Is there anything you can think of that I can do to help him? He's a tough one to read." Jessica eyed her as though trying to figure out what she wanted to say, so Paige reassured her. "I already know about her drug issues. Dr. Seabrook told me when he asked me to work with Will."

Lips pursed, Jessica nodded. "Yes, she definitely had issues but was working through them."

Jessica went on to tell Paige almost exactly what Dylan had shared about Larry and Sandra's new-found happiness. Then Jessica said, "But while she was happy, she also seemed nervous. Kind of like she was always looking over her shoulder. She even mentioned that she might send Will away for a while."

Okay, that was new. "Send Will away? Why?"

"I'm not sure." Jessica took a sip of her coffee. "I don't think she was using again, but she was jumpy. You know she subbed here at the school the day she died."

"No, really?" Paige pretended innocence.

"Yes. We ate lunch together and she was just… I don't know how to explain it. *Jumpy* is the right word." Her eyes narrowed, and she said with a thoughtful frown. "And I overheard her talking on the phone here in the teacher's lounge. We were supposed to get together to talk about going shopping after school. When I walked in, I heard her say something about blackmail."

"Blackmail?" More new information.

"Yes, it was weird." Then Jessica forced a laugh. "So, why are we talking about this, anyway?"

Paige smiled and put on her compassionate-counselor face. "Because you seemed to need to talk. And the more I know about Sandra, the more I'll be able to help Will."

Jessica's face cleared. "Well, I don't know how that'll help, but I hope they find out who killed her."

"The fire was ruled arson, wasn't it?"

Jessica nodded. "Yes. And murder."

The door opened, and Dylan walked in, stopping short when he saw the two women. "Sorry, you look like you're having a pretty deep conversation. I can come back later."

The teacher stood and waved him in. "I was just leaving. My class will be back soon enough, and I need to get some lesson plans written." She looked at Paige. "Thanks for the chat."

Paige walked her to the door.

As the woman left, she nearly bumped into another teacher hurrying down the hall toward the office.

"Oh, sorry," Jessica said.

The other staff member whirled back toward Jessica, the anger on her face making Paige pause. Then the woman said, "I'm getting so sick and tired of things going missing around here."

"What do you mean?" Paige asked while Dylan watched silently.

"I mean, first my ID card grows legs, now a digital camera and a twenty-dollar bill from my desk. Honestly. At least I could replace the ID. But this I'm going to make a stink about. The camera belonged to the school, and the pictures on it were for the yearbook. We've got a thief in this school, and I'm going to report it."

The two women left bemoaning the sorry state of some people who worked in the building.

As they walked off, Paige said to Dylan, "I'm surprised you let Will come to school today."

"He wanted to." Dylan pulled in a deep breath as he fixed a cup of coffee. "I thought about keeping him at home, but when I mentioned it, he went and got his book bag and stood by the door." His eyes softened as he smiled at her. "And I knew I'd be here at the school today and could keep a close eye on him. Plus, Eli promised more security around the school, just in case."

"I noticed the extra cops when I arrived this morning. A couple of Bryson City cars."

Dylan frowned. "I called my secretary and told her I was taking a week off. When I was called to sub for the nurse again, I couldn't pass the opportunity up." He stirred a packet of sugar into the mixture and took a sip. "I was worried that Will being here might put the other kids in danger, but Eli assured me that no kidnapper would try to grab a kid from a class full of students. He said Will is probably safer here than at home. So..." He shrugged and rubbed a hand over his head. "I brought him, and he seemed to be glad to be here. I think he feels safe here."

The door opened again, and the janitor, Sam Hobbs, entered, gave a nod and a smile and went about his business. Soon, he was in the room next door. The smell of bleach reached her nose.

Paige said to Dylan, "I'm going to try and talk to him when he gets finished with his math class."

Gratitude stamped his face. "The more I think about it, the more I believe he saw something the night of the fire."

"But he was unconscious when the firefighters got there, right?"

Dylan nodded. "But he was outside." A shrug. "I just don't know what happened. I don't know why he was outside, why he wasn't in bed. I just…"

His words trailed off and Paige felt her heart hurt for him. "I'll do what I can."

"Thanks." He took a deep breath. "I think I'm going to take him away."

"What?"

"It's too crazy around here." He kept his voice low as his eyes darted to the door. Paige couldn't believe no one had entered and interrupted them. He said, "I think he needs a change of scenery, a place to relax and forget about everything going on here. Saturday, I almost lost him physically. Mentally? Well, I'm sure there's going to be some lasting effects of his attempted kidnapping. He doesn't like to let me out of his sight and…" Dylan's throat bobbed, and he ran a hand across his eyes. "I don't know what I'd do if something happened to him."

Paige placed a hand on his arm. "I understand."

And she did. But she couldn't help the shaft of pain that darted through her at the thought of them leaving.

She stepped back. Dylan closed the distance and pulled her into a hug. "Thank you, Paige."

His strong arms felt like home as they squeezed her, and his light cologne teased her nose. Her heart thumped with the pleasure of being in his arms. Lifting her head, she blinked as she realized his lips were less than an inch from hers.

And she wanted him to close the distance.

But then she remembered that anyone could walk in and catch them. Not that kissing him would be wrong, it just wouldn't be right…here.

A door shut and she jumped. Mr. Hobbs must have finished cleaning the room next door.

Clearing her throat, she stepped back, and his arms dropped. "You're welcome." Where she found the ability to speak, she'd never know.

A slight smile curled his lips, and the look in his eye said she hadn't covered her reaction to him very well. She returned the smile. She didn't care.

Because she knew he felt the same.

"All right," she said, "I'll go get Will and see what I can find out from him."

The light in Dylan's eyes dimmed, and he nodded. "Let me know."

Five minutes later, Paige stood outside Will's classroom door. From her position, she could see

Will sitting in his little desk, his head bent over a paper.

Catching his teacher's attention, she mouthed, "Will."

The woman nodded. "Will? Could you go with Ms. Worth, please?"

Will's head shot up, and his eyes landed on Paige. A smile curved his lips, and he clambered from his seat. Once in the hall, he slipped his hand into Paige's, and together they walked to her office.

Once inside the room, Will planted himself on a chair at the small table and looked at her with expectant eyes.

She sat across from him. "Hey, guy. I was wondering if we could have a little talk."

Wariness replaced his eagerness, and Paige gave an inward wince. But she wasn't ready to stop. Pressing on, she said, "I know things have been kind of scary for you lately, huh?"

His head dropped a notch, but he didn't take his eyes from hers. "Well, I understand that. This big, old world with the big people in it can be kind of scary sometimes. You have every right to be afraid. Especially with everything that's happened to you lately."

Will's shoulders relaxed a fraction.

Paige took heart and kept talking. "You know, you and I have become buddies, haven't we?"

He blinked.

"And I know that when your mom and Larry died in the fire, it was a very hard thing for you."

The shoulders tensed again.

"A very bad person set that fire, Will, and I think your mom and Larry would want you to help find the person responsible for it."

The little boy's forehead creased and his lips tightened. "But if you can't, then I understand that, too. And so would your mother."

At first, Will just sat there and looked at her, his bright, blue eyes probing hers. Then he stood, turned and walked away from her. Defeat sucked the wind from her lungs as she watched him head for the door. Expecting him to keep going, she was surprised when he stopped, turned back to look at her, then seemed to make up his mind about something. Instead of leaving the room, he walked to the small table just to the right of the door and picked up one of the larger, little-boy dolls.

Curious, she watched him.

Clamping a hand over the doll's mouth, Will bent and whispered something into the doll's ear.

Paige stood and moved closer. Slowly, so as not to startle him, she leaned in and tried to make out what he was saying. Only by the time she got close enough, he was done.

Straightening, Will grabbed the doll by the arm

and tossed it to the floor. Sweat stood out on his forehead, and his breath came in quick, shallow pants.

His hands shook and he gulped.

"Will?" She touched his back, and he jerked. "It's okay. You don't have to do anything else, all right?"

Will looked up at her, and she winced at the desperation flashing on his face.

Placing a hand on his arm, she gave him a gentle tug. He collapsed against her and shuddered. Murmuring phrases of comfort Paige rocked him even as her mind processed what he tried to tell her without words.

She had to let Dylan know. Maybe he would understand. For now, she just held the little boy. Once Will calmed down, she pressed him. "Is there anything else you need to tell me? Did you see his face?" He pulled away from her and walked to the door. His little hand twisted the knob and without a backward glance, he began his trek back to his classroom. She watched him walk down the hall, a deputy trailing unobtrusively behind. She waved at him, and he gave her a nod.

Feeling good that Eli was willing to use his deputies to beef up protection at the school, Paige stepped back into her office and wrote down everything Will had done. Each action, every nuance, the expressions on his face, everything she could remember.

A knock on her door snapped her head up. "Come in."

Fiona Whitley. One of the women from the lounge stepped inside. "Hi."

Paige smiled. "Hello."

"We didn't get a chance to talk much the other day. Do you have a minute?"

"Sure, have a seat."

Fiona collapsed into the nearest chair and groaned. "I'm so tired these days. Honestly, if my energy level gets any lower, I'm going to sink through the floor."

Concerned, Paige thought the woman did look rather pale and washed out. "I'm sorry."

Fiona waved aside Paige's sympathy. "I'll be fine."

"Is there something I can help you with?"

"Yes. Dylan is a good friend of mine. We don't see him often enough lately, but I've seen a new sparkle in his eyes since you've come into the picture. In spite of all that's happened to him lately."

Paige lifted a brow, wondering where this was going.

Fiona blushed and said, "I guess what I'm trying to say is he's had a rough time, and I don't want to see him hurt. If you're not..." She trailed off and bit her lip.

Paige's heart swelled. "He's lucky to have you for a friend."

"My brother, Cal, is one of the deputies here in town. He's the one who had to tell Dylan about his sister and her boyfriend."

Paige grimaced. "I'm sorry."

"Working in a small town like this, it's not often a lot of really bad things happen. Well, that was a really bad thing and telling Dylan was one of the hardest things he's ever had to do. And Will…" She shook her head. "I don't know that he'll ever recover."

"He will," Paige said softly. "Somehow, I really believe he will."

Fiona's face softened and a smile graced her pretty lips. "I think I like you, Paige Worth."

Paige grinned. "Thanks. I appreciate that."

Dylan popped his head in, his face grim. When he saw Fiona, he nodded to her but spoke to Paige. "I've got to run over to Bryson City to the hospital. Cheryl's had a heart attack. Do you mind taking Will home and staying with him until I can get there?"

Concern for the woman who was like a mother to Dylan and a grandmother to Will flashed through her. The thought of being responsible for the child sent terror flooding through her. "Dylan, I don't know…"

"Please? He trusts you. I can't leave him with anyone else. Not with everything that's going on."

From the corner of her eye, Paige saw Fiona's brows shoot north. And while the woman didn't say anything, she could almost hear her thinking, *You could leave him with me, with friends you trust and have known for over two decades.*

However, the look in Dylan's eyes said he trusted her. And while part of her reveled in that, her mind mocked, *What makes you think you can be trusted? What if something happens to him the way it did to Ben?* "Sure, I can do that." The words slipped through her lips before she could bite them off.

His relief was obvious. "I'm just going to pop in and make sure everything's okay. I'll be home before dark, I hope. Margaret has a spare key at the office."

Paige eyed him. "And she'd just give it to me?"

"No," Dylan replied. "I'll let her know you're coming."

"Fine. And I have something I need to talk to you about."

His brows creased. "Can it wait?"

Could it? "Yes. I'll tell you tonight when you get home."

"All right. I'll call when I'm on my way."

Dylan left and Fiona smiled. She said, "Be careful with his heart, Paige. I think you already have it in your possession."

She left, and Paige replayed the conversation in her mind. Her stomach clenched when she realized they sounded almost like a married couple. No wonder Fiona's brows lifted.

And then before she could stop the daydream, she wondered what it would be like to be married to Dylan. To fix his dinner, make plans with him…to be a mother to Will.

The last thought shot a surge of fear through her. She remembered the police outside her house when she got back from Mama Ida and Papa Stu's home. She'd only been eight years old, but the police asked her about Ben, wanting to know the identity of the child who had died of pneumonia while her mother ignored his coughing and Paige had escaped to Mama Ida's kind embrace.

Ben's mother had come back for him while the police were questioning Paige, saving her mother from being blamed for the neglect. Ben's mother had been arrested.

Paige still shuddered at the memory. And now she'd just said she'd take Will home and take care of him until Dylan could get home.

She paced from one end of the room to the other. What had she been thinking?

*God? If You're there, and Mama Ida said You always are, would You please help me out here?*

For the rest of the afternoon, she watched the clock, her stomach twisting at the thought of being alone with the little boy who'd captured her heart.

# FOURTEEN

Paige sat on the couch and stared at the television without seeing. Darkness had fallen ten minutes ago. Dylan had called and said he'd be home by seven-fifteen.

She got up, walked down the hall and peered in at the little boy, snuggled under the covers, his arms clutching a ragged stuffed animal.

She'd survived taking care of a child.

*They'd* survived.

Still amazed at that fact, for the first time that she could remember, she felt hopeful. Like maybe she could have a future, be a part of a family. Step out of her lonely existence and share a life with someone.

Stepping across the room to his bed, she brushed his hair back from his forehead and stared down at him. A living, breathing child. And he'd seemed perfectly content to be with her. A miracle.

*Scrape!*

Her nerves jumped, and she whirled to face the bedroom door. Where had the sound come from? "Dylan?" she whispered.

A chill climbed up her spine to lodge itself at the base of her neck. What had she heard?

It wasn't Dylan. He wouldn't just make a noise, then be quiet.

Stepping back down the hall, her gaze flicked to the alarm pad near the front door. Dylan had given her the code, and she'd set it as soon as she and Will had stepped into the house.

It blinked at her in reassurance. Still armed.

Again she wondered where the noise had come from?

Inside?

Outside?

Definitely not inside. No one had set off the alarm.

On silent feet, she padded into the kitchen. Nothing looked disturbed. Leftovers from the pizza she and Will had shared sat on the counter.

Her fingers reached for her weapon, and she took comfort in the feel of it in her palm. Maybe she was overreacting.

Maybe not.

After all of the trauma everyone had been through the past few days, she wasn't taking any chances. It didn't take long to notice the garage door was still shut.

Methodically, she checked each window, fingers giving the locks an extra twist. Satisfaction curled in her. Dylan was taking his security seriously.

Now she stopped. Listened.

Heard nothing.

A glance at the clock told her Dylan would be home soon.

Paige walked back to Will's room where she'd first heard the sound. Without a sound, she moved to the window and checked the lock.

Locked.

Then movement caught her eye. A shadow? Some kind of form skulked beneath a nearby tree.

Two-legged or four?

Darkness hid the details from her.

Adrenaline pumping, she continued to watch, her eyes straining to catch another glimpse of whatever it was that she had seen.

Nothing.

Then headlights swept across the window, and she saw Dylan's car pull into the driveway.

The garage door lifted and still Paige didn't take her gaze from the spot where she felt sure she'd seen someone lurking.

The back door opened and shut. The alarm beeped then was silent. "Paige?"

She tucked her gun away and met him as he walked into the den.

As soon as his eyes landed on her, he frowned. "What's wrong?"

The brief thought that he read her way too easily flickered in her mind. She ignored it and said, "A feeling."

"What kind of feeling?" Wariness flashed.

"Did you see anyone in your yard or lurking around your bushes when you drove up?"

"No, why?"

"I thought I heard something. When I glanced out the window, I thought I saw something. A shadow. It might be nothing."

"Or it might be something. Where's Will?"

"Asleep in his room. I'm going to check out the house. I want you to call Eli and have him come over. We need to talk and I need him involved in this investigation now."

His eyes narrowed. "What are you thinking?"

"I'll tell you when I get back. Call Eli, will you?"

After a brief hesitation, Dylan grabbed his cell phone.

Paige opened the front door and stepped outside.

Once again, Dylan felt helplessness pour over him. If danger lurked outside, Paige could be hurt—or worse. The fact that she was well trained to handle whatever she came across didn't make him feel any better this time than it did the last time.

Eli answered on the third ring.

Dylan quickly explained the situation, and Eli promised to be right over.

While Dylan waited for Eli, he went from window to window, doing his best to keep his eyes on Paige as she walked the perimeter of the house. Everything in him wanted to be out there with her, guarding her back.

But he couldn't leave Will alone. Not when someone had made it more than clear that the little boy was the target.

In Will's room, between glances at Paige through the window, he studied the sleeping child. *Please Lord, keep him safe. Show me how to keep him from harm. Do I take him and run? Stay and fight? Tell me what to do.*

Will stirred in his sleep and his brow furrowed.

Dylan stepped to the window. Even though it was dark outside, the street lamp cast a dim glow on the area around it. He'd lost sight of Paige.

Was evil lurking outside even now?

Watching? Waiting for the chance to snatch the little boy in his sleep?

Was the noise a distraction? A way to get Paige out of the house? Maybe Dylan, too?

Leaving Will unprotected and alone?

Shuddering at the thought but knowing it could

be a real possibility, Dylan pulled a chair close to the side of the small twin bed and took the child's hand in his.

Will rolled toward him but didn't wake.

Where was Paige?

He offered up a short prayer for her safety. For the safety of them all.

He listened for the knock that would signal him to unlock the door and let her in.

Nothing yet.

Had she found something?

Had something—someone—found her?

Agitation clawed at him. Uneasiness churned in his gut.

He had a feeling he should have listened to that still small voice urging him to leave and put Rose Mountain behind him until Paige was finished with her investigation and caught the person responsible for all the chaos going on.

But he hadn't.

Would Will be the one to pay the price for Dylan's hesitation?

Paige kept her weapon out and headed for the spot where she'd last seen the shadow. Wariness and caution shot her adrenaline sky-high. Heart pounding, she paused, trying to listen, straining to hear the slightest sound that didn't belong.

Crickets chirped.

And then a car door slammed. Very faint. Almost indiscernible. And if she hadn't been listening for it, she wouldn't have even noticed it.

Racing in the direction of the noise, Paige knew that she could be facing a dead end. Someone leaving for the night, someone just getting home from dinner.

But instinct sent her to investigate.

Feet pounding the asphalt, she arrived next to a vehicle parked on the street. A look around told her it was the only one nearby. Other cars sat in driveways, but only this one was parked on the curb.

With a perfect view of Dylan's house at the end of the cul-de-sac.

She touched the hood.

Cold. Of course, it would be if the person had been sitting there awhile.

Like while he watched the house.

Her fingers gripped the door handle and pulled.

Locked.

Stepping back, she glanced down the street, then back up.

Eyeing the car one more time, she considered. Had someone gotten out of the car?

Or in?

Did she dare press her face against the tinted, almost black windows to look?

Even now, someone could be on the floorboard, gun pointed toward her. If she got too close…

Paige backpedaled. Probably paranoid, but she didn't feel bad about it one bit. Someone had given her—and Dylan—good reason to be a paranoid.

She took note of the license plate and punched in a text to her boss. Just in case.

Another glance around told her if someone had been outside Will's window, he was gone now.

Paige had started back toward Dylan's house when a car engine started from behind her. She turned in time to see it back from the drive two doors up and speed up the street. The street lamp illuminated the vehicle for a brief moment.

Cold fingers scraped her neck.

She had a feeling the person she'd been looking for had just driven off.

In a white car.

Like the one that had tried to run down Will at the school.

Anxious to get back and tell Dylan she really thought he and Will needed to find a safe place to hide out for a while, she wiped the sweat from her forehead and started toward his house.

The boom shocked her. Froze her in place as the ground rumbled beneath her.

The orange-and-yellow ball rising to the sky

made her run, terrified, horror chasing on her heels, toward Dylan's house where flames now greedily devoured everything in their path.

# FIFTEEN

"Dylan! Will!" Her screams made her hoarse. In disbelief, she stared at the burning house. Her stomach cramped, and she bent double, grief consuming her.

There was no way they'd made it out of there alive.

She started toward the house, ignoring the searing heat. She had to get in there. She had to do something.

A hand on her arm jerked her back.

"Are you crazy?" Eli demanded in her ear.

"They're in there!"

She just now noticed the screaming sound of the sirens. Eli paced forward.

Back.

Rubbed a hand across the top of his head and stared at the flames grasping for the night sky.

"Do something!" she demanded. Tears blurred her vision, and she choked on a sob.

She was DEA. She was supposed to stop stuff like this.

She was supposed to protect them.

And now they were dead.

Because she hadn't done her job and found who was after them.

Paige sank to the ground, flashes of Will's shy smile and Dylan's almost-kiss parading across the forefront of her mind. Along with the memory of the battery he'd replaced for her. His sweet concern. His…

"No-no-no-no. *You can't do this, God,*" she sobbed into her knees.

"Paige."

She wept.

"Paige." The hand on her arm jerked her gaze up to see Eli peering down at her. "Look."

She did.

And saw Dylan walking toward her, Will gripped in his arms.

For a moment, she sat frozen, too stunned to believe what she desperately wanted to believe.

"They're alive?" she whispered. She blinked. They were real. Stumbling to her feet, she flew across the grass and wrapped her arms around both of them, checking for cuts, bruises, burns. "How? Wha—?"

"We were in the car. I felt like we needed to get away. I was going to park down the street a bit, leave Will hidden in the car and come back and get you. I thought whoever was watching the house would think I left again, leaving Will and you in the house. When he went in, I'd follow and…" He flushed. "Dumb plan, huh?"

Dylan held her up against his side. If his arm wasn't around her waist, she wasn't sure her knees would hold her. "No, it was the perfect plan. It saved your lives."

Raindrops splattered her upturned face and she blinked.

He said, "I'd already backed out of the garage when the house exploded. The blast never touched us."

"Will, sweetheart?" She stroked his cheek. "You're okay?"

The boy leaned over and wrapped his arms around her neck.

She gave a choked laugh. "I'll take that as a yes."

Her eyes collided once again with Dylan's. The hand on her waist moved to the back of her head, and he brought her lips to his.

It was rather awkward with Will's arms still clutching her, and for the second time that night, she froze in shock. Then melted into his sweet embrace, her terror at losing him and Will forgotten for a split second. When he pulled back, she couldn't help frowning in protest. Then she saw his eyes on the house.

Squinting through the rain that fell harder.

Will, arms still holding her, whispered, "The bad man said he'd hurt Uncle Dylan just like he hurt my mom."

Paige gasped and her eyes shot to Dylan's. He hadn't heard his nephew's words, they'd been uttered so soft and right next to her ear. She looked back at Will.

"What man?" This time she and Will had Dylan's attention, but she kept her focus on the boy.

For a minute, Will didn't speak again, then he sat up and looked at the firemen putting out the fire intent on destroying yet another of his homes. Head swiveling, he looked at her, then Dylan. "I don't want you to die, too, Uncle Dylan."

Tears filled his eyes and dripped over to splash on his cheeks.

Dylan pulled him into a bear hug. "I know. And I don't want to. Not yet." He stared into the Paige's eyes. "God's stronger than the bad man. He's not going to get me, Will. Understand?"

"Then why did he get my mommy and Larry?"

Paige lifted a brow and wondered how Dylan would handle that one. He looked a little lost, so she jumped in to rescue him, to give him time to think of a response to a question that didn't really have a good answer for a six-year-old who just wanted his mom back.

"Tell me about the bad man, Will." All sounds around her faded as she honed in on Will. Even the rain failed to distract her. Would he tell her or clam up again? In her peripheral vision, she saw Eli standing close by, listening.

Will's eyes darted between her and Dylan. "He said he would hurt Uncle Dylan if I told. He said if I said a word, he'd burn him up just like my Mommy." The little boy's face crumpled. "And I didn't say anything, and he tried to do it anyway."

"So you were protecting your uncle?" He nodded and she rubbed his back. "You're so brave, Will."

"No, I'm not. I was scared. You were brave. You saved me from the car and the bad man who tried to take me from the restaurant."

"Oh, honey." She thought she saw tears standing in Dylan's eyes. Then he blinked and they were gone.

Eli stepped forward, his deputy hat shielding his face from what was sure to be a downpour. "Hey, Will. Glad to hear your voice again, buddy."

Will frowned at the intrusion.

Eli turned to Paige. "You were chasing after the person who did this. Could you ID him at all?"

"No, I…" A thought exploded in her mind. "ID."

"What?"

"It all comes back to that ID found at the fire."

Eli's gaze sharpened. "How do you know about that?"

Paige bit her lip. It was time to come clean. "I'm DEA."

Surprise flashed for a brief moment on Eli's face. "Well, I thought you were something, I just didn't know what."

She lifted a brow. "Really?"

He smiled. "Let's just say I wondered."

"There was an ID found in the fire but it was too badly burned to give us a whole lot of information."

Dylan shifted Will, looked up at the sky. "What do you say we get out of this? Will you two meet me back at Cheryl's house? I think we'll stay there for the night. Fortunately, I packed a small bag for us so we can get through the night. I'll make a final decision about what to do about a place to stay first thing in the morning."

Eli looked at Paige. "There's nothing more you can do here. Why don't you guys go on? I'll be at Cheryl's when I finish up here."

Paige looked at Dylan. "I'll follow you."

With a backward glance at his house, sorrow and grief etched on his face, Dylan gripped Will and headed for the car.

Eli placed a hand on Paige's arm. "We need to talk."

"At Cheryl's house. I think it's time to move in and do some serious investigating into the ID badges at the school."

"Give me at least an hour. I may be able to make it before then."

"You got it."

Paige walked to her car, her thoughts churning, planning.

Praying. *Thank you, God, for sparing them. I didn't realize how much I'd come to care for them until I thought they were gone. I think You're trying to tell me something. Something that I'm afraid to hear.*

She cut the prayer off. While she was grateful beyond words that Dylan listened to the voice telling him to run, real fear settled in her stomach because she was in very deep. Emotionally.

And when it came time to say goodbye, she wasn't sure she would survive it.

Dylan pulled into Cheryl's drive and cut the engine. Will had fallen asleep in the backseat. Climbing out of the car, he walked the few steps to the drain and felt behind the piece of metal. His fingers found the magnetic key holder and he pulled it off.

Sliding it open, he snagged the key and dropped it into his front pocket. He wasn't about to leave

Will in the car while he opened the door. He'd just have to juggle the child against his shoulder while unlocking the door.

The rain had nearly stopped but the heaviness in the air said it wasn't finished for good.

Once inside, Dylan left the lights off, pulled off the boy's wet clothes and replaced them with a pair of pajamas Cheryl kept in the little room Will used when he stayed with her.

All of this, and Will only stirred to mutter a short protest before nodding back off on Dylan's shoulder. Dylan carried him back into the den and placed him on the sofa. The little boy sighed in his sleep, but his forehead was smooth. Like he'd given himself permission to rest without fear anymore.

Just speaking the words, sharing the burden he'd been carrying around inside him for so long with the adults he trusted seemed to give him a new measure of peace and security.

Soon he saw headlights flash across the front window and figured Paige had arrived. However, he wasn't ready to take that for granted. Walking to the window, he looked out.

As his pulse hummed, he watched Paige climb from the vehicle with a glance to the sky. The kiss they'd shared at his house seared his mind. He'd seen her grief, her weeping because she thought he and Will had been in the house during the explosion.

And he knew she cared. Probably much more than she wanted to admit. He saw the love in her eyes when Will hugged her.

But loving a child was different than wanting to take on the full responsibility of parenting one.

She rapped on the door and he opened it.

And handed her a towel.

Paige took it with a smile. "Thanks."

"Will's asleep on the couch," he told her. "I'm just not ready for him to be out of my sight yet."

"I understand." She kept her voice soft.

"If we sit in the kitchen, I can still see him and maybe our voices won't disturb him."

She nodded and set her keys on the kitchen counter. Dylan walked to the cupboard and pulled down a coffee filter. He added water to the maker and pressed the button to start the process.

Soon the smell of fresh-brewed coffee filled the room.

When he turned back to Paige, her gaze slammed into him.

And he sucked in a deep breath.

Realization came fast and not necessarily wanted at that moment.

He loved her. He loved another woman who wouldn't be able to commit to him and Will.

Now what was he going to do?

\* \* \*

He looked shell-shocked. Who wouldn't after this night?

"How's Cheryl?" she asked.

Blinking, Dylan shook himself. "Awake and holding her own. I checked on her on the way over here. Let her know that something had happened with my house and asked her if she minded us staying here."

"And of course she didn't."

He smiled. "Of course."

Paige finally asked the question that she'd been meaning to ask for a while now. "Where are you parents, Dylan? You've never said."

"They died within a year of each other. Mom of cancer, Dad of a heart attack." He sank into the chair next to her.

She clasped his fingers. "I'm so sorry. Recently?"

He squeezed back. "No, about six years ago. Right after Will was born."

"No wonder you were so protective of Sandra."

He nodded. "I tried, but she was already hooked by the time Will was born. It's a miracle he was born so healthy. I don't think she was doing cocaine at that point. That stuff came later, but still…"

"Where's Will's dad?"

Dylan shrugged. "I don't know. Sandra got married right out of high school. He took off, and about year later, she was pregnant with Will." Sadness filled his eyes, and her heart went out to him.

"I'm sorry," she said.

A knock on the door brought Paige to her feet, hand on her gun.

Dylan stood and said, "It's probably just Eli."

It was.

Eli entered the kitchen and took a seat at the table. Dylan sat opposite him, and Paige found herself in the middle.

Eli looked at her, leaned back and crossed his arms. "Can you fill me in?"

She looked at Dylan, back to Eli, and started talking.

After she'd brought him up-to-date on everything with the case, she said, "So, as you know, the only evidence found in the fire was a school ID that had all of the information burned off except partial letters of the elementary school's name."

"What about Larry and Sandra?"

"Larry was undercover in the high school. He was subbing as a math teacher. The man was a whiz with numbers. Anyway, he said he met Sandra in the teacher's lounge one morning and could tell she was on something." Paige shot an apologetic look at Dylan who blinked and looked away. "To make a long story short, he fell in love with her, convinced her to get clean, trust him and give him names of those involved with the drug running. She told him about the two elementary school parents who'd been arrested on drug charges, but didn't know who the top dog was. That's what Larry was working on finding out when he was killed."

"So that's two connections to the elementary school. The parents and the ID tag," Eli murmured.

"Right. Which is why we decided to focus on the elementary school rather than the high school."

Dylan's eyes sharpened. "Then you need to figure out which staff member is missing an ID."

"We tried that. Two people reported lost IDs and had replacements made, but they checked out clean."

Eli paced to the kitchen and perched on a bar stool. "Could the ID belong to a past employee who just happened to have it on him at the time of the fire?"

Respect for the sheriff blossomed. "We thought about that, too. The dates on the ID were still discernable. They were for this year."

Dylan interrupted. "The two people who were questioned about their missing badges, did they say what happened to them?"

"One went boating and dropped his wallet in the lake. He never did recover it. We checked that story and it was legit. He applied for a new license, new credit cards, everything."

"And the other?" Eli asked.

"She said she left her badge in the top drawer of her desk like always. One day it was there, the next it was missing."

"That wouldn't happen to be the day after the fire, would it?"

Paige nodded. "The very one."

"Okay, so a staff member—" Dylan started.

"—or a very clever volunteer—" Paige interrupted.

"—stole the badge and now has access to the school," Eli finished.

"Right." She nodded and took a sip of water.

"I suppose changing the locks and codes for the cards are out of the question," Dylan muttered.

"Too expensive. The school doesn't have the funds for that kind of thing." She'd thought about that herself and looked into the cost. It was astronomical. Way too costly for a school already hit hard with cutbacks and layoffs.

Eli glanced at his watch. "First thing in the morning, we're going to take care of this."

"The only way to do that is to check every staff member's ID card. That teacher's missing badge keeps ringing in my mind. What if the person who killed Larry and Sandra lost his badge at the scene of the murder? He sure wouldn't want to report the fact that it was missing."

Dylan caught on to her line of thinking. "So he stole a badge and forged himself a new ID using some kind of computer software."

"Right." Paige nodded. "All he would have to do is place his picture and name on the badge. Duplicating the barcode on the back would be way too complicated unless he has some super-sophisticated equipment."

"But as long as he has the stolen one, he can put anything on the front, and it'll work just fine."

"And as long as no one looked too close, it would be very easy to get away with it," Eli muttered. "Of course, this is all speculation, but it makes sense to me. I'm going to bring in some officers from Bryson City to be on standby. However, I don't want that school in a panic."

"And we sure don't want to tip off the wrong person that we're searching. We'll have to be subtle," Paige agreed. "Make up a story about key cards needing to be reprogrammed due to some kind of technical glitch in the system. Whatever. The guidance counselor often helps out in different situations. No one would question me taking their key card and returning it 'reprogrammed.'"

Dylan rubbed his eyes. "I'm taking Will away from all of this. I'll let him sleep in late in the morning, then we're going to take a little trip out of town."

Paige felt a crack in the vicinity of her heart. She understood Dylan wanting to leave, but she sure didn't like it.

The plan made, Eli left with admonitions to keep him in the loop from now on. By the time Paige touched base with Charles and filled him in on everything, it was pushing ten o'clock.

Dylan looked like he'd been hit by a truck. She probably did, too.

"Please say goodbye before you leave tomorrow." Her throat clogged on the words.

And then she was in his arms for the second time that night. She breathed in his scent, a mixture of smoke and cologne. And maybe some leftover fear.

His hand cupped her head and brought her face up to his. "I don't want to leave you."

"But have to. For Will. I know and I understand."

"We'll be back."

Paige nodded and felt his fingers slide through her hair to massage her scalp. Closing her eyes, she let her muscles relax as his hands moved from her head to her shoulders, to her upper arms, then back up to her neck.

His lips touched hers once. Twice. She let her

arms slip around his waist and rested her head on his chest. "God answered my prayers tonight."

"Mine, too."

"Thank you for showing me how to find Him again."

She felt him smile against her hair. "He wasn't lost."

Paige felt her lips turn up. "I know. I was."

"Be careful tomorrow. Whoever tried to kill us tonight isn't playing games."

"I'm the cop, remember?" she chided him.

"A cop I care about. A cop Will trusted enough to break his silence with."

Paige bit her lip and looked in the direction of the den. She hadn't forgotten about Will. But it seemed like all of her reasons for staying away from Dylan and Will were being deleted one by one.

Especially her argument that she would make a lousy mother. Dylan didn't believe that.

And Paige was starting to wonder if she'd been wrong all these years. That she *could* have a family. That she *could* be a better mother than her own mother had been. That she *could* forgive herself for Ben's death.

Dylan held her for a few more moments, then gently escorted her to the door. "Get some sleep. Morning will be here before you know it."

Sleep. Right. She had a zillion things to do in

preparation for tomorrow. Instead of telling him that, she looked in the direction of the couch.

"Where did Will go?"

# SIXTEEN

Dylan's breath lodged in his throat as he spied the empty couch. "Will? Where are you?"

No answer.

"Will?" Paige joined in. Moving from room to room, they searched the house and came up empty.

Panic clawed at Dylan even while he told himself to calm down. "There's no way someone got in here and snatched him. We were right there. All the doors were locked…"

Raking a hand through her already mussed hair, Paige clamped her lips tight. Fighting tears, he thought.

"No, no one got in, Dylan. I think Will left voluntarily."

Incredulous, he stared at her. "Why would he do that? He knows someone is trying to hurt him."

"I don't know." She walked to the sliding-glass doors just off the den. "Look. They're unlocked."

"But I went through the house checking windows and doors, making sure they were—"

"That's what I'm saying, Dylan. Will let himself out. Call Eli and tell him what's going on. I'll go after him."

Dylan stopped her move to open the door. Reaching behind him, he grabbed the cordless and placed it into her palm. "It's your turn to call. I'm going after Will."

He left her punching in Eli's number.

Sliding the door open, Dylan stepped onto the deck, ignored the pouring rain and raced down the steps to the backyard.

He stopped and looked around. Did he dare call out for the little boy? What if someone had followed them to the house? If Dylan yelled Will's name, that person would know Will wasn't in the house.

If he didn't know it already.

Dylan ran around to the front of the house, then stopped.

He glanced up the street, then back down. It was hard to see anything in the pouring rain. The darkness didn't help, either.

Which way would Will go?

*Where* would he go?

The front door opened, and Paige loped down the steps to join him on the street. "Any sign of him?"

"No. Is Eli on the way back?"

"Yes."

"Should we split up?" Dylan wondered aloud as he desperately tried to decide the direction he should take.

"First, you need to talk to me. Where would he go?"

"I don't know." Frustration and worry filled him. "I was just asking myself that question a minute ago." He threw his hands up. I can't think of a special place for him. Where he would go for comfort." Dylan cut his eyes to Paige. "Maybe to your place."

She lifted a brow. "But I'm here."

"I know. I'm desperate. Grasping at straws."

"How far did your sister live from here?" Paige asked him as Eli's car pulled into the drive.

"About a mile."

"So it's pretty reasonable that he could walk that," she muttered.

"Yeah, but it's all uphill. Sandra and Will lived next to one of the trailer parks not far from the little church on the hill."

She rubbed her eyes then nodded. "All right. Then you and I will go that way while we send Eli in the other direction."

Walking over to the police cruiser, Dylan leaned in and explained the situation. The words rushed from him as his adrenaline surge urged him to hurry and start looking for Will.

Windshield wipers going full speed, Eli backed from the drive with the promise to call if he found anything.

Dylan turned to Paige. "Let me get a flashlight, then we can go."

When he returned, they headed in the direction of Sandra's house. Dylan wondered if the person after Will had already snatched the child from the dark street. He shuddered and determined not to think along those lines. Not until he had some sort of proof.

Right now, the evidence said Will had wandered off on his own.

But was someone waiting for a chance to take him? Were they searching in vain?

*Please, dear Lord, please keep him safe.*

"How often does he stay with Cheryl here?" Paige's questions interrupted his stream of never-ending prayers.

"Often enough to be comfortable, to know the neighborhood. He passed it every day for six years to get to his home when Sandra was alive."

"So he knows the way."

"Definitely."

Dylan's already-elevated blood pressure notched up as he scanned the darkness. Trees on either side of the lonely road rose up like skeletons wavering in the downpour, reaching out, mocking him, telling him Will was forever lost.

He went back to his prayers, pushing aside the taunting voices, shoving down the raging fear, and concentrated on not missing one detail of the area around him.

They walked in silence, just the crunch of their shoes interrupting the quiet. Rain pooled around the collar of her raincoat and dripped down her back. By the time she reached their destination, she would be soaking wet.

"Should we call for him now that we're away from the house?" Dylan asked Paige.

"Yes, I think that might be a good idea."

A car approached, and Paige shoved Dylan to the side of the road behind a large tree as the headlights grew closer. "Do you recognize the car?" she asked.

"No, not yet. I can't see it well enough."

"Then let's stay out of sight until you can."

Tires whooshed on the mountain road and Dylan froze, feeling the heat radiate from Paige— as well as tension. She kept her hand on her gun, waiting and ready.

Finally, the vehicle was almost on them.

And Dylan took his first deep breath in minutes. "That's Cal."

"Cal?"

"One of the deputies and a good friend of mine," he said as he waited for the right moment to make his presence known.

"Oh, right. Fiona's brother."

Dylan stepped out and flagged down the deputy.

Cal pulled up beside them. "I got the call from Eli about Will going missing. Thought I'd check up here."

"That's where we're headed," Paige said.

"Want a ride?" Cal offered.

"No, thanks," Dylan said. "We're checking the woods on either side of the road. He may be scared. Hiding out."

Cal nodded. "I'll head on up to the house and see if he's there. I've got your cell number if I spot him."

Cal drove off and Dylan's jaw tightened. "Will! Where are you?" he hollered.

He heard the desperation in his voice, but couldn't do anything about it.

Paige's fingers curled around his and squeezed her support.

"I can't lose him, Paige. I'll never forgive myself if…"

"We'll find him. We have to."

Her quiet words strengthened him. "Pray for him," he asked.

"I haven't stopped since we saw he was missing."

Dylan's heart throbbed with conflicting emotions, aching for his nephew. And glad Paige seemed to have found her peace with God.

"Please Lord…" he whispered. And couldn't force another word past the huge lump in his throat.

"Amen," Paige ended. Dylan looked at her. She shrugged and gave a watery smile. "God knows our hearts and our pain. He'll fill in the blanks."

Dylan squeezed her to him in a quick hug, his emotions near to overflowing. Then he stepped back, and they continued their search.

Paige didn't get it. Why would Will leave the safety of the house? What was he thinking? As they approached the charred remains of Sandra's house, the full moon helped light the way. Paige's eyes scanned the area. "Will? Honey, are you here? Where are you?"

Cal's car pulled up beside them. He rolled down the window and said, "I haven't seen any sign of him. But there's tornadic activity headed this way. I think an active tornado might touch down for real this time."

Dylan's face fell at the first part of Cal's news, hope sliding off to crash and burn. At the second part, worry reappeared.

Paige nodded her thanks, and Cal said, "I'll drive on past aways. Maybe once he got here and realized no one was here, he kept going."

Dylan pulled in a deep breath. "Thanks, Cal."

Cal drove off and the world fell silent, broken only by the sound of the pouring rain.

Paige shifted, the hair lifting on the back of her neck. Had they been followed? Squinting through the water, she caught movement to her right. "Look," she said.

Dylan looked. "What?"

"I saw something over there." Not taking any chances, she freed her weapon from the shoulder holster and motioned for Dylan to slip behind the nearest tree. He frowned, took her by the upper arm and pulled her with him. She went, eyes still on the area where she thought she'd seen something, but the rain made it hard to make anything out. "Will? Your Uncle Dylan is here. Why'd you leave the house? We're very worried about you." To Dylan, she said, "Keep talking to him."

"What if it's not him?"

"Then whoever's in those bushes will think *we* think it *is* Will, and I'll be able to surprise him."

Without giving him a chance to protest, she kept to the cover of the trees and started making her way around to the other side of the property.

More movement about a foot away from where she'd seen the first sign they weren't alone.

She heard Dylan calling reassurances to Will.

Paige crept closer.

And closer.

Then paused to listen. Dylan's voice echoed. Sniffling? Or the rain?

Just a few more steps brought her close enough to see a small form huddled against a tree, face buried in his knees.

Paige closed the distance on silent feet and dropped to her knees beside the boy. "Will," she whispered.

His head snapped up and anger flashed across his face. "No! You're not supposed to find me!" Will hopped to his feet and started to race off.

Paige shot out an arm and caught him around the waist. In much the same way that she'd done the day she'd swept him from the path of the car. "Hold on, little guy. I thought we were friends. I thought you trusted me." She said the words loud, hoping Dylan would hear her and realize she'd found Will.

"I do trust you! But the bad man won't leave us alone."

Confused, she simply stared at Will for a minute, trying to wrap her mind around his six-year-old logic. "I know the bad man seems to be winning, but I think we're going to catch him tomorrow."

"Uh-uh. You're not. And he's going to kill Uncle Dylan." His little face crumpled and sobs ripped from him to stab her in the heart more effectively than if he'd used a knife.

"Will, Will, what are you saying?"

"He is, he is," he hiccupped through his sobs. "But if he has me, he'll leave Uncle Dylan alone."

And she understood.

She looked up in time to see horror cross Dylan's face. Rain sluiced down his face as Dylan dropped to the ground in front of his nephew and wrapped his arms around the child's quivering frame. Paige shivered, just now realizing she was chilled. The temperatures hovered in the mid-seventies, but with wet clothes and hair, she was cold.

"Will, what are you saying?"

Will lifted tearful, blue eyes and met his uncle's gaze. "He told me if I said anything about that night, he'd kill you. He said it. And I believe him now. He blew up the house to the sky and—"

Dylan gave a choked cry and pulled Will into his arms. "He's not going to get me. Or you. We're going away. Far, far away from the bad man, okay? First thing in the morning."

Will stilled, sniffled. "Where are we going?"

"Someplace safe. Someplace where you can be a kid and be happy again, all right?"

The child seemed to think about that. His gaze flicked back and forth between Paige and Dylan. "But what about Paige?" he asked, his voice low.

Dylan's eyes met hers, his filled with an emotion she was almost afraid to try and identify.

"When Paige catches the bad man, she'll let me know, and we'll come home, okay?"

"And see Paige again?"

"You'll see me again, Will. I promise." Paige leaned in to hug him and plant a kiss on his cheek. "One way or another, you'll see me again."

"And Uncle Dylan will be safe?" He drew in a shuddering hiccup.

She nodded, the tears clogging her throat, making her swallow twice before she could speak. "Totally safe. And you, too. No more worries, no more scary dreams, no more being afraid."

Will slipped out of his uncle's embrace, and Paige felt him slide his little arms around her neck. She squeezed him tight, smelling his sweaty, little-boy smell—and relishing it. Cherishing it. Holding tight to it.

*Please, Lord, help me keep my promise.*

Then he was back in Dylan's arms. She pulled out her cell phone, swiping off the tears and the rainwater with the back of her hand. Once she could see well enough, she dialed Eli's number. Fortunately, she had a pretty good signal even as high as they were on the mountain.

"Hello?"

"We found him."

"Then get somewhere safe! There's a tornado in the area!"

# SEVENTEEN

"Dylan! We need a place to take cover. A tornado may be touching down nearby!"

Dylan held up a hand and closed his eyes. "Hear that?"

"Sounds like a train." She knew what that meant. Growing up, Mama Ida warned her if there was ever a tornado predicted, and she heard something that sounded like a train, to find a safe place.

Like a basement.

Only they didn't have a basement.

"We need to get out of here!" Another kind of fear took over as she realized that the bad guys might win after all. Thanks to an act of nature.

"Follow me!" Dylan hollered as he grabbed the flashlight and pointed it in a direction only he seemed to know that would lead them somewhere.

Without question, she grabbed the wrist that held the flashlight and ducked her head against the deluge. Will grabbed Dylan's neck in a choke hold and held on while his uncle raced toward a place Paige couldn't see.

But he'd grown up here. He knew this mountain. And she trusted him.

With her life.

Pounding past the burned shell of his sister's house, he ran toward the trees.

The train came closer.

Wind whipped her hair into her eyes and across her cheeks, stinging her skin.

And still they ran.

She heard Will crying, Dylan's reassuring yell that it was going to be okay.

Her breath whooshed out as she hit a particularly rough group of branches. She yelled a warning. Dylan would knock himself unconscious before he'd let go of that little boy.

"There!"

She saw where he was headed.

A bridge.

The noise grew louder. Closer.

Together they fought the increased winds, pushing, straining to reach their goal even as the wind fought back, struggling to keep her from safety.

"Please God," she whispered in a pant. "You've brought us this far. Don't let go of us now."

Branches whipped around her. One slapped her across the back, and she gasped at the pain spiraling up her.

Another caught Dylan in the side of the head, and he reeled, blood dripping from the gash.

"Are you okay?" she yelled at him.

"Fine! Go! Go!" He stayed hunched over the child in his arms, protecting him for the flying debris, even as his other hand pulled on hers.

She ran.

"Get under the bridge!"

She dove under, hit the ground—and the ankle deep water in the creek the bridge covered. "Oomph."

She felt Dylan fall beside her. His breaths came in pants. "Climb up underneath as far as you can."

Scrambling, grasping at whatever she could get her hands on, she pulled her way up. Wood finally surrounded her as she sat huddled, shivering.

Dylan stumbled up next to her, holding tight to Will. With the flashlight still working, she could see the little boy tremble, the tears on his cheeks. *Dear Lord, hasn't he been through enough? Please get us out of this alive.*

Reaching out, she grasped his hand. "It's going to be fine, little guy, okay?"

He nodded and gave her a tremulous smile.

She prayed like she'd never prayed before and thought she could see Dylan's lips moving. The flashlight bobbed in his hand.

And then all was still.

The sudden silence seemed loud, making her ears ring.

Dylan's raspy breaths filled her ears.

And then, once again, she felt his lips on hers.

She kissed him with all the relief she felt at being alive. With all the love she had pent up begging for release. Whether she would admit it or not.

And then his arms closed around her, bringing her as close as possible with Will still squished between them. Will's sudden giggle was the best thing she'd heard in her life.

The resilience of children.

"Is it over?"

She squeezed him again. "Sounds like it."

Dylan's breath puffed over her left ear. "Let's go home."

Together, they crawled out from under the bridge and surveyed the mess left by the storm.

Fallen trees and scattered debris lay before them, highlighted by the weak light of the flashlight.

"Wow," Paige breathed.

"And that was a small tornado," Dylan agreed.

"It's going to take some work climbing over all this stuff."

"I wonder how the town fared," he murmured.

"Maybe it just hit the mountain."

"Let's go find out."

\* \* \*

Paige rose early and dressed without thinking about it. They'd discovered that the town had fared remarkably well. In fact, the tornado had only hit the little mountain with minimal damage and no casualties.

As a result, life went on.

And so did their plans for the day.

Her mind went to Will's actions from the night before. The little boy had been willing to place himself in the hands of the bad man in order to save the uncle he loved.

She marveled at the fact that a six-year-old would understand the concept of sacrifice like that. Shaking her head, she clipped on her badge in a place that would keep it hidden until she needed to pull it out and shove it in the face of the one wreaking havoc in the lives of those she loved.

She froze.

Loved?

A tremor shook her. Okay, she had to admit it. She loved them. The little family had wormed its way into her heart and taken up permanent residence. And the tornado had made her finally face it. She'd almost lost it all last night. Not just her life, but Dylan and Will. The thought made her nauseous.

So what did that mean for the future? For her and them?

She wasn't sure. "Just focus on catching the killer first. Then you can worry about your future."

Saying the words aloud spurred her on to the school where Eli would meet her. They planned to sit down with the principal and fill him in on everything. From all of her observations, Tom Bridges was innocent of any wrongdoing going on in his school. His background check had come back clean even before she started this assignment.

She wished she had a specific suspect that she could zero in on, but she didn't. Checking the IDs was her only hope right now.

Once in the principal's office, she asked, "How many staff do you have out today?"

The shock of who Paige really was had yet to wear off, but thankfully, Tom Bridges managed to gather himself together and be a help and not a hindrance. He whirled his chair to the computer screen and tapped a few keys. Then he said, "We have four teachers absent."

Eli said, "Write down their addresses, if you don't mind. I'll have my deputies go out to their homes and request permission to check their IDs."

Principal Bridges did as requested and handed the short list to Eli. The sheriff excused himself and stepped from the office to call it in to the deputies.

Paige said, "We don't want anyone to know

what we're doing. I'm going to go room to room and ask for the badges to 'reprogram.' That way the students remain calm and none of the teachers suspect anything. We do have extra security and police surrounding the area and in the building undercover posing as parents and volunteers. They've already gotten their badges and are in position."

Principal Bridges nodded. "All right. What else do you need me to do?"

"If we find what we suspect we'll find—a tampered ID badge—then whoever it belongs to may not surrender quietly. We'll need to make sure the classrooms can be locked down immediately if necessary."

"They can be. We have lockdown drills."

"Good. But that's a last resort. We're going to try and do this peacefully, with no one the wiser."

Pulling in a deep breath, the man nodded and stood. "All right. Anything else?"

Paige stood beside him. "No sir, I think that'll do it." She gazed at him. "I'm sorry for the deception. We just felt like we didn't have a choice in this matter."

"I understand. I don't like it, but I do understand."

Paige smiled her relief. "Thanks."

She stepped out of his office, adjusted the gun under her arm and went to work.

\* \* \*

Dylan settled Will into his car seat under the watchful eye of Deputy Callum McIvers. Eli had asked him to make sure they got safely out of town. Only then would Cal report to the school to be ready in case he was needed.

Dylan climbed into the vehicle, looked back at Will, who gave him the first real smile in a long time. "We're out of here, dude. Okay?"

Will gave him a thumbs-up. Dylan took that as a good sign.

Then a frown crossed the little boy's lips. "Wait. I gotta go to school."

"What? Why?" A glance in the rearview mirror showed Cal following at a distance.

"'Cuz I forgot to tell Paige something."

"But Paige is busy catching the bad man, remember?"

The jaw so much like his own jutted at him. "I gotta tell her."

"Tell her what?"

"Is she gonna get hurt?"

"I…no…she's not."

Tears welled up in Will's eyes. "I gotta tell her! You have to let me! Please, take me to school. Nothing bad ever happens there."

Exasperated, Dylan couldn't decide what to do but this was obviously very important to Will.

"Can I just call her and let you talk to her on the phone?"

"No! I gotta see her!"

The sheer desperation on Will's face made Dylan pause. This wasn't a normal, run-of-the-mill demand. This was something Will felt very strongly about.

What did he do?

"If I take you, I'm getting your books and all your work. We'll pop in the office, then right back to the car, okay?"

Will palmed the tears away and calmed down. "Okay."

Dylan shook his head. He couldn't fathom what was going through the child's mind and was really too tired to try and figure it out at the moment.

Finally at the bottom of the mountain, he turned right and headed toward the elementary school.

At the stoplight, he pulled his cell from the cup holder and dialed Cal's number.

The cop answered on the second ring. "What you need, Dyl?"

"I need to stop at the school."

"That's probably not a good idea."

Dylan launched into the explanation of why. Grudgingly, Cal acquiesced and followed them into the parking lot of the school.

By this time, Dylan had dialed Paige's number

twice with no answer. Slipping his phone into his pocket, he climbed out and got Will from the car.

Looking around the school, everything appeared normal. A parent exited and nodded to him. Dylan forced a return smile and held Will's hand as they walked through the door.

At the front desk, he greeted the secretary. "Good morning. Could you let Paige know we're here in the office? Will would like to say something to her before we take off for a few days."

"She's been awfully busy coming back and forth, reprogramming the IDs. Why don't you have a seat and wait on her?"

Dylan didn't want to wait. Everything in him was ready to get on the road and get out of this town that had almost destroyed his entire family. He looked down and froze.

Will was gone again.

This time exasperation hit him. He could see he was going to have to have a little talk and reinforce that Will needed to stay with him and not just walk away any time he felt like it.

Worry niggled inside him, but not the raging fear he'd felt when Will had disappeared last night. This was Will's school. He was comfortable here.

Dylan just had to look in a logical place, find the child, then get out of town.

Simple enough. Dylan walked out of the office and went to locate his wayward nephew.

However, no matter how much he tried to reassure himself that Will was fine, he couldn't help the niggling sense of foreboding that he was walking right into trouble.

Paige handed the badge back to Jessica, hiding her frustration. She'd been in and out of every classroom, "reprogramming" badges. Each one had been tamper-free.

Jessica thanked her. "I haven't seen Will today. Is he all right?"

"He's fine," Paige assured her. "He and Dylan are just taking a little trip this week."

"He's missing school?"

"Just a few days."

Jessica shrugged and walked back into her classroom.

Children scampered past Paige in the hallway, a few stopping to give her a hug. In spite of her frustration at her lack of success in finding a tampered badge, she smiled. She'd made some friends here.

Paige pulled the list of staff members from her back pocket and checked off Jessica's name. The last deputy had reported in. The four absent staff members' badges had also not been altered. She checked those names off.

Six names left. Including office and mainte-
nance staff.

"Any luck?"

Tom Bridges rounded the corner, new lines on
his face suggesting he wasn't dealing well with
the stress they'd laid on him today.

"No, sorry, not yet. Six more."

She showed him the list. He nodded. "I'll take
these three, you get the last three. Sam Hobbs is
waxing the cafeteria floor, Lila Johnson was vac-
uuming the library and Stacy Dobson was sweeping the back hall."

"Got 'em." The cafeteria was two doors down.
She'd start there.

Dylan ground his teeth, his anger at himself
barely under control. How had Will managed to
slip off again?

Exasperation consumed him. He looked at the
secretary. "Did you happen to see which way Will
went?"

"Toward his classroom, I think."

His classroom and Paige's office were off the
same hall. Adhering the name tag to his left shoulder, Dylan exited the office and headed toward
Will's classroom. He'd stop in at Paige's office
and see if she was there.

Looking in the door, he was almost shocked
to find it empty. He'd fully expected to see her

and Will in conversation, Will telling her whatever he'd been so adamant about stopping by the school for.

"Huh." He turned and made his way toward Will's classroom.

Paige watched Eli approach, his footsteps moving him down the hall at a rapid clip. The look on his face didn't bode well. "What is it?" she asked.

"Right after the accident with Alex, I had my deputies start running plates of every white car they came across to see if it matched up with anyone that might be a potential suspect." He grimaced. "You wouldn't think there would be that many in a town this size, but there are. That's why it's taken us so long."

"What'd you find?"

"I started matching white cars to cleared badges. There's only one left that hasn't cleared."

"Whose?"

"Sam Hobbs."

She blinked. "The janitor? Is his car in the parking lot right now?"

"Nope. He's got a red Ford truck he just purchased about two months ago. That's the one in the parking lot." He gave a tight smile. "However, the white car hidden in his shed in the back has a damaged front headlight."

She drew in a deep breath. "Okay, that's pretty much enough evidence for me. However, let's find him and check his badge just for good measure."

"Working on it now."

"Hey, Paige."

She turned and gaped. "Dylan? What are you doing here?"

"Is Will with you?" His words were tense, and she could hear the frustration behind them.

"No. I thought you two were on your way out of town."

Worry flickered across his face. "We were. Then Will insisted we stop here. Had a fit that he had to tell you something. I stopped to sign in at the desk. When I turned around, he was gone. Again."

"You find him. And stay away from Sam Hobbs. He may be the one we're looking for. He owns a white car with a damaged headlight."

"Sam?"

"Yeah. Plus we haven't cleared his badge yet."

"I'll keep an eye out for him."

Paige saw the glint in his eye and laid a hand on his arm. "I'm not saying he's the one. I'm saying be careful." She looked at Eli. "I'm going to go with my gut. Can you have one of the deputies start a background check on him? Let's move

Sam to the top of the priority list and track him down. He's still innocent until proven guilty. Just because the car's in his name doesn't mean he's the driver."

Eli nodded and glanced at his list. "I will say that the others still to be cleared don't own a white car."

"At least not in their name."

He shrugged. "True."

"Still, I'd feel better if we cleared Sam first."

Dylan raked a hand through his hair. "I knew I should have just kept going."

Paige gave him a gentle shove in the direction of Will's classroom. "See if he's there. If he is, wave at me from the door, get him and get out. I can give you five minutes, so please just grab him and go. We're going to have to put the school on lockdown just in case the person we're looking for turns out to be Mr. Hobbs and he turns ugly."

Dylan nodded. "Five minutes. That's all I need." He spun on his heel and headed for the classroom. Paige waited until she saw his relieved face look back. He gave a wave and disappeared back into the room.

Will was safe.

She looked at Eli. "Where was Mr. Hobbs last seen?"

"The cafeteria."

"Let's start there."

\* \* \*

Dylan pulled Will into a hug. "Why didn't you wait on me, buddy?" Without giving Will a chance to answer, Dylan looked at Will's teacher, Ms. Conley. "I just brought him for a minute. When I looked back, he was gone."

"Um, that might be my fault." Ms. Conley gave him a sheepish smile. "I saw him in the office. I motioned him to come with me. I thought you were just bringing him late and were signing him in."

It didn't matter. Will was safe, and that was all that mattered. Now, it was time to leave. They needed to hurry.

He told Will, "I just saw Paige. She's really busy, so we'll have to see her another time, okay?"

"No! I have to see her now." Will pulled back.

Dylan felt helplessness fall over him. "What's so urgent, Will?"

"I have to tell her something."

"What?"

"I have to tell her—"

The door opened and a voice called out, "Hi, Ms. Conley, I've got a little something from the office that needs to go home with…"

Dylan turned and saw Sam Hobbs standing there, envelope in his left hand, eyes locked on Will.

# EIGHTEEN

Paige waited until she felt sure Dylan and Will had enough time to leave, then requested the school be put on lockdown. If she was wrong about Mr. Hobbs, she'd apologize.

However, her gut kept insisting she was doing the right thing. The only problem is they would have to go room to room once again in order to enforce the lockdown. If there was a Code Red announced over the PA system, Mr. Hobbs—or the person responsible—would be put on alert and go into hiding.

And while he didn't know that they were on to him yet, the Code Red might make him nervous. Nervous enough to do something stupid. And Paige desperately wanted to avoid that.

When people did stupid things, other people, innocent people, usually ended up hurt.

She went classroom to classroom explaining they had an intruder on campus, and everyone was to stay in the classroom keeping the door locked until further notice.

When Paige got to Jessica's room, the woman frowned at her. "Is everything all right?"

"I'm sure it will be. Just keep the door locked, all right?"

"Sure." The woman shut the door and Paige moved on.


Dylan shoved Will behind him as he stared at the man Paige thought was behind the terror inflicted on his family. The man who may have murdered his sister and Larry.

And because Dylan had been too slow to leave town, he had placed Will—and the rest of the students in this classroom—in danger.

If he was overreacting, he'd apologize later.

Dylan felt his body react to the adrenaline rushing through it. No one else seemed to be disturbed by the man's presence. Mr. Hobbs set his mop against the wall and shoved the bucket to the side of the door. His fingers clutched the white envelope he'd pulled from his pocket upon entering the classroom.

All the while, he kept his eyes on Dylan and Will.

Eyes that had narrowed at Dylan's protective move.

And Dylan realized his mistake.

He'd automatically moved to protect Will when Sam entered the room. Realization flashed across the man's face.

Dylan cleared his throat and tried to bluff. "We were just leaving." He turned to Ms. Conley. "We'll see you the beginning of next week."

He pulled Will beside him, not wanting the child to know anything was wrong and moved toward the door.

The janitor let Dylan and Will pass him, then followed them into the hallway. The door clicked shut behind him.

"We were just leaving," repeated Dylan, praying Sam would let them leave without making a scene.

Instead, the man looked up and down the hall then back at Dylan and Alex. Dylan realized how empty the hallway was between them and the exit.

When the man pulled a gun faster than he could blink, Dylan froze.

"You're not going anywhere," Sam growled at Dylan. "I guess the gig's up, isn't? Your first reaction to seeing me is to hide the kid. That says a lot."

Dylan backed up. "What are you doing?" Terror made his words choppy.

"What I've been trying to do all along. Get rid of you and the kid." Sam backed them up to Paige's office and motioned with the gun. Dylan followed the command, keeping himself between Will and the gun. Still holding the weapon steady, Sam used his other hand to grab the keys from his pocket and open the door.

If it had just been him, Dylan would have taken the chance and jumped the man, but he couldn't do that with Will there.

Keeping his face toward Sam, Dylan managed to scoot Will into the room behind him, never allowing the gun to be aimed at the boy. Sam shut them in Paige's office.

"Why?" Dylan asked. "Why get rid of us?"

"I overheard you talking in the lounge about how you and that counselor were going to be talking to him about the fire. But even before that, I know he saw me that night."

Dylan gulped. "But he never saw your face. He couldn't have identified you."

The man's eyes narrowed. "I'm not so sure about that. Just a few days ago, he looked at me like he recognized me."

"Probably your guilty conscience."

"Shut up," Sam snarled. "I've been sneaking around this school, trying to avoid that kid for long enough. And I simply couldn't take the chance that he would keep his mouth shut forever. I don't know what he saw me do. I would have killed him that night, but the cops got there fast. A neighbor called it in before I could finish the job."

Keep him talking was all Dylan could think of. Find a way to get the gun. "So you just had time to warn him to keep his mouth shut."

"Yeah." He glared at Will. "And we see how well that worked."

Dylan searched for the right thing to say, anything to get the man's focus off Will. Dylan felt Will moving behind him. He pressed his fingers against the boy's arm, hoping he would get the message to be still.

Sam waved the gun and muttered, "I can't believe this."

An indrawn breath behind Dylan made him turn and look down at Will. The child's face was bleached white. His lips worked as he stared at the janitor.

A knock on the door made them all jump.

"Who's in there?" Paige's voice came from the hallway. "Will? Dylan?"

He pointed the gun at Dylan, then back at Will. "You better tell them everything is just fine."

"But everything's not fine!" The words burst from little Will and echoed through the room. "You're the bad man! You killed my mom and Larry!"

"Will! Who's in there?" Paige's voice came clearly through the door.

"The bad man, Paige!"

Dylan kept a desperate hold on the child struggling to launch himself at the man he'd just realized was responsible for his mother's death.

"Will, be still!" Dylan ordered.

Will was beyond listening at this point.

Sam watched, seemingly mesmerized by the child's anger.

And then Will was free, slipping out of his uncle's grasp as his little T-shirt ripped.

Horror filled Dylan as Will ran to Sam and lashed out with kicks and punches. "Will! Stop!"

Sam grappled with Will as he tried to pull the gun around and gain control of the situation.

Dylan crept closer, waiting for the right moment, praying one would present itself.

More banging and yelling from the outside. He registered the panic in Paige's voice.

Saw the gun turn toward Will.

And Dylan launched himself between the two, his elbow clipping Will in the chest and his left hand snagging the wrist of the hand that held the gun. All three crashed to the floor. The door slammed open.

And the gun went off.

Paige's terror knew no limits as her ears rang from the sound of the gunshot. She leveled her gun at the now struggling men. "Freeze!"

An officer slipped around her, snagged Will from the floor and bolted out of the office.

Paige's eyes followed Dylan and Sam as they rolled, ignoring her order. "Freeze! And I mean now!"

Eli came in beside her, his weapon trained on the struggling duo. She couldn't get a clear shot.

Then she saw Sam move, his weapon aimed at Dylan's head and for a brief second, she had a shot.

She took it and the weapon bucked in her hand.

Sam screamed and dropped back, Dylan landing on top of him. Sam's gun skittered across the floor.

Eli pounced, kicked the weapon aside.

Paige shoved Dylan off, landed a knee in Sam's back, and pinned him to the floor. Within seconds, she had his hands cuffed and Sam in Eli's custody.

Now her concern shifted. She zeroed in on Dylan who sat on the floor, back to the wall, getting his bearings. "Will," he whispered as his gaze became frantic, searching, probing, looking for the child he loved.

Paige hurried over and laid a hand on his arm. "He's fine. He's with Cal."

Dylan slumped back.

"Hey, I need a doctor!" Sam's voice penetrated.

She looked up and saw her bullet had plowed into his right shoulder. Exactly where she'd been aiming.

She glared at him. "You'll live."

"No thanks to you," he spat back.

Turning her back on him as Eli shoved him from the room, she focused back on Dylan. "Are you hurt anywhere?"

He shook his head. "Just my pride."

"Excuse me?"

"It was pretty stupid of me to bring Will back here just because he insisted." Tears appeared for a brief moment before he blinked them away. "I don't know if I'm cut out for this whole parenting thing," he whispered.

"What?" His statement rocked her. "What do you mean? You're one of the best parents I've ever seen. You're fantastic with Will."

He shook his head again. "I messed up. Big time. So big I endangered his life."

"Not on purpose. This whole thing was supposed to be low-key. It was supposed to be look at the badges, see which one had been tampered with—if one had—and then question the person it belonged to. Simple."

"I know. But I also knew the person responsible had killed before. Might very well be a staff member at this school. And I just didn't… I didn't make the right decisions."

Her heart went out to him. "You can second-guess yourself, Dylan. But either way, Will needs you."

Dylan took a deep breath. "Yes, he does. And by the grace of God and with His help, I'll get the hang of this parenting thing one day at a time."

"Yeah, I believe you will."

"I need to see Will now that I've stopped shaking."

"Come on." She held out a hand and he grasped it.

An officer stood to the side guarding the scene until a forensics team could get there. He nodded that he would handle the situation for now. Paige smiled her thanks, and together, she and Dylan went to find Will.

Dylan's heart thumped when he saw Will held in Cal's arms. A lump formed in his throat as he realized it was finally all over. He held out his arms, and Will fell into them. Dylan pulled the little boy close and breathed in his scent. "It's over, buddy. The bad man is in jail. He can never hurt us again."

Will pulled back and stared into his uncle's eyes. "For real?"

"For real."

Paige watched them, and he thought he saw tears in her eyes. He looked at Will. "What was so important that you had to tell Paige?"

A shy smile crossed the child's face, and Dylan wondered what was going on in that head of his. Will held out his hand toward Paige, and she grasped it. Will's smile slid off, and he frowned. "I got mad at my mama. She told me I couldn't have a puppy."

"I'm sorry," Paige offered, but looked confused.

"The night the fire burned up my house. I was mad at her so I ran away. Only it was cold so I came back." Tears filled his eyes and dripped over onto his cheeks. He swiped his eyes and sniffed. "But when I got back, the fire was really, really bad. I yelled and yelled for her to come out, but she didn't. Then the bad man grabbed me and told me not to tell anyone anything. He'd hurt Uncle Dylan if I said a word. So I didn't say anything."

"Oh, honey," she whispered.

"What about Paige, Will?" Dylan pressed.

"I didn't tell my mama I loved her. I did that morning but not that night. I was going to tell her, but it was too late." He looked at Paige. "I didn't want it to be too late for you."

Paige's eyes went wide. "What?"

"I wanted to tell you I love you, Paige."

Dylan thought he heard a sob escape her. Then she choked, "Oh, Will, I love you, too, honey."

A bright smile spread across his sweet face, and Dylan's breath left him in a whoosh. He looked at Paige. "I love you too, Paige."

She gaped and swallowed. Fear flashed before she could hide it. Dylan felt his heart sink. She pulled in a deep breath. "Excuse me, I…I need to go question Sam Hobbs."

His hand shot out and grasped her wrist. "We need to talk."

"I know," she whispered. Then she gently twisted out of his grasp, spun on her heel and walked away.

# NINETEEN

Paige looked up to see Dylan enter the police station. Her heart shifted in her chest, and she realized she wanted to jump up and throw herself in his arms.

But fear gnawed at her gut.

When Will had said he loved her, her heart had felt like he'd grabbed it in both hands and given it a squeeze. When Dylan had said he loved her, she'd just flat-out panicked. No one other than Mama Ida and Papa Stu had ever said those words to her. Twice in one day was almost more than she could process.

So, what was Dylan doing here? The determined look on his face made her push aside her notes.

"Where's Will?"

"He went home with Fiona. She said he could stay with her until I could get him. He knows Fiona, loves her like another aunt. I told him I'd be back soon—with you."

She swallowed hard. "I see." No sense in getting into that now. She knew they had to talk; now just wasn't the time. "So, what are you doing here?"

His jaw jutted. "I want to hear what Sam has to say. Have you questioned him yet?"

"Not yet, but—"

He held up a hand. "Don't even try to keep me out of it."

She glanced over at Eli who'd been studiously ignoring the two of them. "Paperwork that interesting, Eli?" she asked.

Without looking up, he said, "Yep."

"So, what do you think? Can Dylan watch from behind the mirror?"

Eli shrugged. "Why not?"

Satisfaction crossed Dylan's face. As well as relief. He was worried she'd flat-out refuse. As well she probably should, but he and his nephew had been the targets. She figured he probably deserved to observe if he wanted to.

She nodded to Dylan. "You can go ahead and have a seat in the observation room. We'll get started in a few minutes. They had to patch him up at the hospital, but they're en route now."

Dylan's eyes studied her for a brief pause, then he nodded and headed in the direction she pointed.

"When are you going to put that man out of his misery?" Eli spoke the words to his paperwork.

"Excuse me?" she asked.

Now his eyes met hers. "He's as in love with you as you are with him. When are you going to quit denying it?"

Paige felt heat suffuse her face. "I don't know what you're talking about."

Eli leaned forward. "Look, I've been in his shoes. Crazy about a woman who's crazy about me but too scared to do anything about it. Don't let your fear rule your life."

She gaped. "How—"

"Don't ask how. Just ask yourself if you really want to be alone the rest of your life. And if it's worth letting fear be your guide rather than the Lord." He stood and winked. "Now, I'm done with the paperwork—and the lecture. See you in the room in a few."

Paige stared as he disappeared around the corner, then gathered her scattered wits and prepared to confront a killer.

Dylan watched her enter the interrogation room and wondered how their story would end. *God, You know how I feel about her. She knows how I feel about her. I think You want us together, I'm just not sure she gets it. Tell me how to help her get past the fear she has.*

The short prayer was all he had time for before

Cal turned up the volume. Dylan was grateful for his friend's presence.

Paige leaned against the table, silent but watchful. She didn't speak, just stared at Sam Hobbs.

The man stared back. Began to fidget.

And still she stared.

"What?" Sam finally blurted. "Quit staring at me! If you've got questions, ask them."

"Your partner squealed on you," she finally said.

The man jerked like she'd slapped him. "Wh-what?"

"Yeah, gave you up. Told us how you were in charge of the drug ring. All of it."

"No way. I don't believe you." But the sweat popping out on his forehead said he considered it a real possibility.

"Doesn't really matter if you believe it or not. Doesn't make it any less true. So—" she looped her fingers together in front her as though she didn't have a care in the world "—are you going to take the fall by yourself or try to cut a better deal than your partner?"

Rivulets of water ran from his brow. He wiped his cheek on his sleeve. "You don't have anything."

"I don't know, Sam, I think we have quite a bit." Sarcasm bit. "Dylan will testify that you admitted to wanting to get rid of Will. Now, to keep this all legal and everything, you were offered a lawyer when you were arrested. You refused. I think now might be a good time to call one."

His face went slack. "You want me to call a lawyer?"

"Is this guy for real?" Dylan asked Cal. "Does he think that by denying everything, it'll just be forgotten?"

"You'd be surprised what some criminals think," Cal answered.

"Oh, yeah," Paige was grinning at Sam in a way Dylan hoped she never did with him. An I-gotcha-where-I-want-you-and-now-you're-toast smile. "I want to make sure this is all legal and everything. You're not getting off on a technical-ity on my watch."

Sam narrowed his eyes in an effort to look like he didn't care. His shaking hands gave him away. "I don't want a lawyer," he mumbled. "I didn't do anything."

"Except enter a school with a gun."

"It was an accident. I thought my life was in danger."

Paige burst out laughing. "Okay. You go with that one."

"You don't have anything on me!" The shaking hands slapped the table.

Cal said to Dylan, "He's crazy. I can't believe he hasn't lawyered up." Cal pointed to the recorder on the table. "Anything she manages to get out of him is admissible in a court of law."

Paige leaned forward and got nose-to-nose with the man. "We've got you on an attempted murder several times over. You came into a classroom with drugs in your hand. Then you pulled a gun." She gave a laugh that said she couldn't believe how stupid the man in front of her was.

Then she backed off and shrugged. "I guess your partner's going to enjoy all the money y'all made while you're sitting behind bars." She smirked, then sobered. "Personally, I don't care what you do. We'll give the deal to your flunky, and you can do the hard time." Paige headed for the door, her stride confident, her attitude stating she didn't have time for Sam's nonsense and she was done dealing with him.

"Wait!" Sam called just as her fingers twisted the knob.

She waited, her back to him. "Give me something."

"What did she say?" Sam blurted.

From where he sat, Dylan watched the satisfied smile spread across her lips before she wiped it off and turned back to lift a brow at Sam.

"Man, she's good," Cal whispered.

"What do you mean?"

"She never used a pronoun the whole time she referred to his accomplice. She didn't know whether the person was male or female so she worked around it."

Dylan had more questions—like how she knew there was someone else involved—but didn't want to ask. She was talking again.

Paige rubbed her palms together as she walked back to lean against the table again. "She said a lot. Said it was all your idea to funnel the drugs through the school. Said you came up with the idea of how to get them past the drug dogs." She gave a ferocious frown and pulled an envelope from her pocket. Slapping it down in front of Sam, she snarled, "Sending drugs home in kids' backpacks? That's low. Killing a kid's mom and boyfriend? That's life in prison."

Red fury erupted on his face. Fists slammed down on the table in front of him. "That stupid, big-mouthed—"

Paige interrupted him. "Yeah, she had a lot of nice things to say about you, too."

Sam fumed. Dylan thought if the man grew any redder, he'd blow a vessel.

Paige pulled out the chair across from Sam and flopped into it. "So, you ready to start talking or not?"

"What kind of deal are we talking?"

"Well, I can't make the deal. I'll have to get the A.D.A. in here."

"Then get him in here."

Paige turned to the door when Sam spoke again. "You don't have her, do you? That was a bluff. How did you know?"

"About your partner?"

"Yeah."

"It was only a guess, but I knew for a fact you couldn't be in two places at the same time."

He frowned. "What do you mean?"

Paige shrugged. "The night I went to the school to snoop around, someone was there in the hall. Was that you?"

Sam nodded.

"Then your partner was at Dylan's house looking through the window, scaring Will."

Sam scowled. "She was just supposed to be getting the layout of the house."

"Like where Will's room was so you could set off a bomb under his window in an attempt to kill him?"

The man's eyes never wavered, but the nervous tic in his cheek said she'd hit the nail on the head. "I'd be interested in hearing what the D.A. has to offer now."

Paige wanted to wipe the smarmy look off the man's face. A man who'd just admitted to killing Sandra Price and Larry Bolin. And a man who had threatened to kill Dylan if Will told what he saw that night.

Which actually turned out to be nothing.

But who was his partner? All she knew was that it was a woman. She didn't want Sam to turn his partner in to cut a deal. She wanted him fully punished.

Eli opened the door and waved her out. "What is it?"

"We've been through his apartment and found the evidence that we needed. We know who his partner is."

"Who?"

"Jessica Stanton. She thinks Sam ratted her out and is singing like a songbird trying to make sure she gets as little time in jail as possible."

Paige let herself into her house for the last time. Her heart felt heavy—and yet numbness spread through her. The doctor had called her this morning.

Her mother had died this morning on her couch shortly after placing a call to 911. When EMTs arrived, the woman was gone.

She'd died alone. No family gathered around her. No one to mourn her passing.

Paige blinked back tears. Was she destined to follow right in her mother's footsteps after spending her life doing her best to make sure she was nothing like her mother?

The thought made her stomach cramp.

Pulling in a deep breath, she focused on another depressing thought.

She was done here in Rose Mountain. The good thing was that she'd completed her job, done what she came here to do. Sam Hobbs and Jessica Stanton had turned on each other like rabid dogs, trying to pin as much of their operation on each other as possible.

Jessica had made up the whole thing about Sandra saying someone was blackmailing her. And it was Sandra confiding to the woman she thought was a friend about how she was going to have a new life with her new boyfriend that had gotten her and Larry killed. Sam had been spooked that Sandra knew too much and had gotten rid of her. He'd gotten lucky as Larry had been there, too. The pipe bomb he'd tossed through the window had been quick and deadly.

Sandra and Larry hadn't stood a chance.

But Paige had done her job, and now Larry's family and Dylan could have closure.

And she could go back to Atlanta and get on with her life.

Without Dylan and Will.

The thought sent a shaft of pain through her. She didn't want to leave Rose Mountain. It had become her home. She'd found love here. The love of God and a family.

It had become her refuge.

"God," she whispered to the empty room, "how am I going to leave here?"

And deep down she knew she didn't have to. All she had to do was pick up the phone and tell Dylan she wanted to spend the rest of her life with him and Will.

But could she do it? Could she make that commitment? What happened if she was a lousy mother? Will was better off with no mother than a bad one, that was for sure. What if she repeated her mother's mistakes? She had done it once before. *But you were only eight.* Could she forgive herself?

She grabbed her suitcase and walked to the front door. One last, lingering glance, and she relived each moment with Dylan and Will. Then packed away the memories for the lonely days ahead.

Opening the door, she stepped outside.

To find Dylan and Will sitting on the hood of his car.

She gaped, her heart tumbling wildly in her chest.

"Paige!" Will was the first to move. He hopped down from the car with Dylan's help and hurled himself toward her like a bullet.

Her throat clogged as she gathered him in a hug. "Hey, guy, how are you doing?"

"I'm doing great! Look! I lost a tooth!"

She grinned at his enthusiasm. "My goodness, how much money did you get for it?"

"Ten whole dollars!"

"Ten? Wow, that's a lot more than I ever got."

She lifted her gaze to Dylan who waited patiently. He now leaned against the car, watching them, the expression on his face hopeful, longing.

And sad.

As though he knew he wasn't going to change her mind.

But, oh, how she wanted to. To just shove aside the fear and let herself believe Dylan when he said she'd be a great mom. To believe in herself. To believe God when He said He works all things together for good for those who love Him.

"We couldn't let you go without saying goodbye."

"I... Thanks."

Will jumped up and down. "We got you a present, too."

"You did?"

"Uh-huh. Don't you want to know what it is? 'Cuz I'll tell you if you want. You don't hafta guess."

Paige felt the laugh well up, and her eyes collided with Dylan's. "Why don't you show me?"

Will ran around to the back of the car. "Open the trunk, Uncle Dylan."

Dylan pressed a button on his remote, and the lid popped up.

She walked around and looked in. And gasped. Her heart melted. "Seriously?"

"Seriously." Dylan reached in and pulled the bicycle out. "What do you think?"

Tears blurred her vision, and she sniffed. "Oh, you guys. It's just perfect. Thank you."

"So, you really like it?" Will's eyes were brighter than any child's on Christmas morning.

"I really do."

"We don't want you to leave, Paige. We want you to stay. With us." Dylan's voice softened. She could see his heart in his eyes as they bored into hers.

She pointed to the swing in her neighbor's yard. "Hey, Will, why don't you go swing a bit while I talk to your uncle, okay?"

"Will you push me?"

"In a few minutes."

He bounded off, and Paige took a deep breath. She walked over to Dylan, who opened his arms.

As though it was the most natural thing in the world, she slipped into them, felt them close around her.

Breathing in his clean scent, the smell of his cologne once again surrounding her, she lay her head on his chest. "My mom died this morning."

His sharp, indrawn breath echoed in her ear as he pushed her back to look in her eyes. "I'm so sorry."

He placed a kiss on her forehead, and she felt a tear trickle down her cheek.

"I'm sorry, too. Sorry I couldn't do anything for her."

He pulled her back into a tight squeeze. "It's not your fault." Dylan's sympathetic rumble almost made her smile. Almost.

"I don't want to be like her. All alone. Afraid to love anyone after the way she was treated by most of the men in her life. I don't want to be like that." She paused. "I don't want to leave, but I'm afraid I don't know how to be a mother." Softly she told him about Ben and how guilty she felt for not saving him.

The arms around her tightened. "Have faith, Paige. God brought you here for that very reason. So that you could see that your maternal instincts are good. Will loves you."

His husky plea sent her heart spiraling, pounding. "I'm scared," she whispered. "Scared I'm not good enough. Scared I can't get over my past."

"I know. But if you run from us, from your future, you'll always be scared. Stay and fight for us. Face your fears, and you'll find you had nothing to fear in the first place."

She shuddered, then gave a shaky smile. "The

way you made Will stay at that restaurant and eat even after he'd almost been snatched?"

Dylan nodded. "As much as I wanted to pick him up and run out of there, never to return. But that would be silly because that's being scared of something that can't hurt you."

"But failing you and Will *can* hurt me," she whispered. "And not just me, it can hurt two people I've come to…care about very much."

He placed a finger under her chin to bring her eyes up to meet his.

The love there sucked the air from her lungs.

"You know, God doesn't want us to be afraid. He actually wants to give us the desires of our heart, keeping His will for us in sight." He placed a light kiss on her lips. "I believe God sent you into our lives for a reason. Not just to get the bad guy tormenting us, but because God had a more permanent arrangement in mind."

"You think?" She wanted to believe it.

"I think. You're amazing with Will. I know you doubt your parenting, but all parents do. You have nothing to worry about."

"But I—"

"That's not to say you'll be perfect. Any more than I'll be the perfect dad. We're human. We're going to mess up. But we'll be leaning on God, trusting Him to guide us—and probably asking for forgiveness and more guidance. A lot."

"Dylan, I—"

"And—" he placed a finger on her lips "—one of the things I know about you is that you'll protect that child with your life. Before you knew him, you could have died trying to save him. You put his life before yours. What other qualifications for motherhood does one need?"

She ran out of protests. He was right. She would die for either one of them. Emotion swelled inside her.

*What do I do, God?*

Staring into the eyes of love, she felt peace rocket through her. Not that the fear totally left her, but she finally wanted something more.

And she knew what she was supposed to do.

"Okay. I'll stay. I'll give us a chance."

His eyes shot wide. And his jaw dropped.

She laughed and pulled his lips to hers. After one of the sweetest kisses she'd ever experienced, Dylan grabbed her in a bear hug, lifted her up and swung her in a circle. "Yes!"

Will came running over, excitement lighting his eyes. "Did you ask her, Uncle Dylan? Is she going to marry us?"

Her heart stilled as Dylan planted her feet back on the ground. A smile graced his lips. "Well, I was going to take it a little slower than that. Not that I'm in doubt, but I didn't want to push you.

However, that's where I'd like to end up. With you in a white dress."

"And I get to wear a tux with a green bow tie." Will grinned up at her.

Nearly overwhelmed with emotion, she hauled in a deep breath. "Green?" was all she could think to say.

Will shrugged. "I like green."

A laugh burst from her, and she reached out to snag him into the circle of love.

Turning serious, she stared at Dylan. "I'm not easy to love."

His smile never wavered. "I'm willing to take my chances."

Paige looked down at Will. "Okay, I guess you're stuck with me."

Will let out a whoop and shot his fist into the air.

Dylan grinned down at her. "I think he approves."

The smile stayed on her lips as she stared up at him. "I know I don't want to lose you, Dylan. But I have to be honest. I need to take it slow."

He nodded and let his forehead tap hers. "Slow is fine. It's a chance, and that's all we're asking for."

Tears welled up and fell over onto her cheeks. "I can do that."

# EPILOGUE

*Two years later*
*May*

"He's got my hair, Mama Paige. Ow! Make him let go."

Paige hurried into the den and couldn't hold in the giggle. Eight-year-old Will lay on the floor beside David, his six-month-old baby cousin.

The infant had tangled his little fingers in Will's shaggy head. David now tried to bring those strands into his open mouth.

Paige gently released Will from the hold, and he rolled away rubbing the sore spot on his head. His lips split into a grin. "He's strong."

"I know. Gotta be careful around those fingers, kiddo."

David rolled over onto his stomach and kicked his legs. Soon he'd be crawling, then walking. Then running.

Looking at her two boys, love overwhelmed her, choked her up and made her grateful all at the same time.

The door shut and Will popped up to race into his uncle's open arms.

Paige picked up David before he could scoot any farther off the rug and placed him on her hip. His hand went straight for her hair.

One hand wrapped around his well-padded rear and the other holding his hand so he didn't leave a bald patch, she walked into the kitchen to find Dylan on his knees looking Will in the eyes. They looked very serious.

"What's up, guys?" They started and looked at her. Suspicion narrowed her eyes. "What are you two planning?"

Will broke into a giggle, and Dylan gave a sheepish grin. "We need to get ready if we're going to church."

She frowned. "I would love to go, but you've had a really long night. I know you're exhausted."

"Not too exhausted to go to church with my family."

For the first time, she noticed his hand behind his back. "What are you hiding?"

Another laugh from Will. Another grin from Dylan.

"Um. Nothing?" Dylan teased.

"Uh-huh, I'm not buying it. What do you have?"

"Show her, Uncle Dylan, show her!"

Will's excitement fueled hers. What was her husband up to?

With a flourish, he pulled his hand from behind his back and presented her with four red roses. Dylan bounced on his toes. "There's four. One for each of us."

Paige felt her heart swell. "Aw. That's really sweet."

Dylan leaned over and placed a kiss on his son's head, then one on his wife's lips. He smiled down at her and said, "Happy Mother's Day, Paige."

She let the tears flow over. Her first Mother's Day. Her eyes bounced back and forth between Dylan and Will and baby David. "Yeah, this is my first Mother's Day with David, but—" she passed the baby to Dylan and dropped to her knees in front of Will "—when you opened your heart to me and loved me, you made me feel like a mother even before David was born." She reached out and drew him to her. "Thank you so much for that, Will. I love you very much."

"I know. I love you, too." The child hugged her back then skipped off into the den.

Paige looked at Dylan. "Thanks for not giving up on me."

"Thank you for not giving up on yourself."

"I probably would have if you hadn't come along."

He grinned. "God knows what we need when we need it. I'm glad He decided to use me."

Paige laughed. "You're going to remind me of that often, aren't you?"

"Yep."

"Cool."

And with one hand still holding the baby, he wrapped the other around her shoulders to place a kiss on her lips, and Paige reveled in the place she now called home. Dylan's arms.

\* \* \* \* \*

Dear Reader,

I do hope you had as much fun reading this story as I had creating it. It was a thrill to revisit Rose Mountain (the little North Carolina town first created in the novella Dark Obsession—February 2010). Dylan and Paige made such a great couple, I found myself cheering for them as they fell in love. And Will, ah, yes, little Will. I hope you thought he was as adorable as I did. True, he suffered a horrible trauma, but because of a whole lot of love, patience and counseling, he came through everything a fighter. I just loved that about him. A funny thing about the little boy in this story—I was writing and my nine-year-old son came in to read over my shoulder as I worked. He does that sometimes. And I said I had to change the name of the little boy in the story for various reasons. My son looked at me and said, "Use my name." Then he gave me that dimpled grin. How could I say no? So, the little boy in the story became Will.

Paige had a lot of fear in her life. Her fear almost made her lose out on a great guy and future full of love and happiness. I hope that if you're dealing with some kind of fear that's keeping you from enjoying life to the fullest, you'll give it to God and take that leap of faith that God Himself wants you to have life and have it more abundantly.

God bless!

*Lynette Eason*

# QUESTIONS FOR DISCUSSION

1. In the opening scene, Paige risks her life to save little Will Price. As a result, it created a bond between the child and Paige. How do you feel about that? Would you be willing to die for a child you didn't know?

2. Can you make that particular scene symbolic? A representation of Christ's love for his children?

3. In the beginning of the story, Paige must deceive Dylan about her true identity. How do you feel about that?

4. Paige was a real loner in life. No real friends other than those she worked with, and even then, she didn't let anyone get too close. What do you think it was about Dylan that made him special? How did he get past Paige and her armor?

5. One of Paige's biggest concerns was falling for a man who wanted children. She was determined she'd never be a mother because she was afraid she'd turn out just like her own. Did you feel her fears were well-founded? Did you identify with her inner conflict of loving

Dylan and Will, but being afraid of failing them, too?

6. Growing up, Paige's saving grace was the couple in her neighborhood who selflessly gave of themselves. They fed her body *and* her spirit. As a result, Paige was able to believe in herself and that she could rise above her circumstances to make something out of her life. Do you know people like this? What do you think would happen if more people displayed God's love in this manner?

7. What was your favorite scene? Why?

8. Who was your favorite character and why?

9. What did you think about Paige's job as a school counselor? Did you think it was a good cover for her?

10. I fell in love with Will Price. What did you think of his character?

11. Were you able to figure out who the villain was? If so, what gave him away?

12. Paige wanted to be a mother. But she was afraid. When she finally let it go, gave it to God, she found a new freedom. Has that ever

happened to you? What are you afraid of? Can you give it to God and find freedom in being rid of that fear?

13. Do you live in an area that is at risk for tornadoes?

14. Do you fear natural disasters and weather occurrences? How can you overcome that?

15. If you were in Will's position, what would you do and why? Would you keep silent to protect others or tell?

# LARGER-PRINT BOOKS!

**GET 2 FREE
LARGER-PRINT NOVELS
PLUS 2 FREE
MYSTERY GIFTS**

*Love Inspired* ®
SUSPENSE
RIVETING INSPIRATIONAL ROMANCE

## Larger-print novels are now available...

**YES!** Please send me 2 FREE LARGER-PRINT Love Inspired® Suspense novels and my 2 FREE mystery gifts (gifts are worth about $10). After receiving them, if I don't wish to receive any more books, I can return the shipping statement marked "cancel". If I don't cancel, I will receive 4 brand-new novels every month and be billed just $4.99 per book in the U.S. or $5.49 per book in Canada. That's a saving of at least 23% off the cover price. It's quite a bargain! Shipping and handling is just 50¢ per book in the U.S. and 75¢ per book in Canada.* I understand that accepting the 2 free books and gifts places me under no obligation to buy anything. I can always return a shipment and cancel at any time. Even if I never buy another book, the two free books and gifts are mine to keep forever.

110/310 IDN FEH3

| | | |
|---|---|---|
| Name | (PLEASE PRINT) | |
| Address | | Apt. # |
| City | State/Prov. | Zip/Postal Code |

Signature (if under 18, a parent or guardian must sign)

Mail to the **Reader Service:**
**IN U.S.A.:** P.O. Box 1867, Buffalo, NY 14240-1867
**IN CANADA:** P.O. Box 609, Fort Erie, Ontario L2A 5X3

Not valid for current subscribers to Love Inspired Suspense larger-print books.

**Are you a current subscriber to Love Inspired Suspense books
and want to receive the larger-print edition?
Call 1-800-873-8635 or visit www.ReaderService.com.**

\* Terms and prices subject to change without notice. Prices do not include applicable taxes. Sales tax applicable in N.Y. Canadian residents will be charged applicable taxes. Offer not valid in Quebec. This offer is limited to one order per household. All orders subject to credit approval. Credit or debit balances in a customer's account(s) may be offset by any other outstanding balance owed by or to the customer. Please allow 4 to 6 weeks for delivery. Offer available while quantities last.

**Your Privacy**—The Reader Service is committed to protecting your privacy. Our Privacy Policy is available online at www.ReaderService.com or upon request from the Reader Service.

We make a portion of our mailing list available to reputable third parties that offer products we believe may interest you. If you prefer that we not exchange your name with third parties, or if you wish to clarify or modify your communication preferences, please visit us at www.ReaderService.com/consumerchoice or write to us at Reader Service Preference Service, P.O. Box 9062, Buffalo, NY 14269. Include your complete name and address.

LISUSLP11B

# LARGER-PRINT BOOKS!

## GET 2 FREE
## LARGER-PRINT NOVELS
## PLUS 2 FREE
## MYSTERY GIFTS

*Love Inspired*™

### Larger-print novels are now available...

LILP11B